SUMMER'S END

Other books by R.D. Skillings:

Alternative Lives, 1974, stories

P-town Stories (or The Meat-rack), 1980

In a Murderous Time, 1984, stories

Where the Time Goes, 1999, stories

How Many Die, 2001, novel

Obsidian, 2001, novella

Memory for Marisa Rose, 2003, poems

Many thanks to the magazines that first published these stories:

NOTRE DAME REVIEW
"The Rights of Salvage," "The Other Party," "What Befell Her,"
"Nothing Happens Again," "Pills," "The World to Come"

SOUTH DAKOTA REVIEW
"Once at Summer Camp"

SHANKPAINTER
"The Girl Who Saw God"

AMOSKEAG
"Ten O'Clock in the Morning"

TRIQUARTERLY
"The Blue Stone" (as "The Ivory Tower")

HAWAII LITERARY REVIEW
"In the Dunes" (as "The Sand Pit")

NORTH DAKOTA REVIEW
"The Tomb of Hiram Gooms" (as "Never the Sign of a Star")

CAPE COD VOICE
"Noon in the Old Colony Tap, 2005"

NOSTOC
"The Bed"

SUMMER'S END

stories by
R.D. Skillings

PROVINCETOWN ARTS PRESS
a nonprofit press for artists and writers

Provincetown Arts Press
650 Commercial Street, Provincetown, MA 02657
www.provincetownarts.org

Cover painting: Jane Kogan, *Portrait of Roger Skillings in Front of the Fo'c'sle*, 1969, oil on canvas, 79.125 by 36.25 inches, copyright the artist

Cover and book design by Irene Lipton
Back cover author photo by Phil Smith

This book is funded in part by the Massachusetts Cultural Council, a state agency that also receives support from the National Endowment for the Arts.

Library of Congress Control Number: 2016935878
ISBN: 0-944854-60-5

∞   The paper used in this publication meets the minimum requirements of the American National Standard for Information Sciences—Permanence of Paper for Printed Library Materials. ANSI Z39.48-1992.

PRINTED IN USA
1 2 3 4 5 6 7 8 9 10

To Marshall Brooks and William O'Rourke

Table of Contents

◇◇◇◇◇◇◇◇◇◇◇◇◇◇◇◇

Introduction

◇◇◇◇◇◇◇◇◇◇◇

In June of 1966, when he was twenty-nine years old, living in Boston, R.D. Skillings fell in love with Provincetown at first sight. After three summers there, he moved to Provincetown year-round in May of 1969 and won one of the first seven Fellowships in writing at the newly established Fine Arts Work Center, then a fledgling organization founded to support visual artists and writers at the early stages of their careers. A native of Bath, Maine, Skillings has lived in P-town year-round ever since.

Located at the extreme tip of Cape Cod, Provincetown is a place both minuscule and vast. It has been home, in the course of its history, to Native Americans, Pilgrims, fishermen, immigrants, outcasts, homosexuals, makers, visionaries. Those who know it know this rich, eclectic broth. They know the insular embrace of Commercial Street, the barren sweep of the dunes, the wildness of the surrounding sea. They know that it is a place whose beauty both beckons and bewilders, a place where creativity thrives.

For forty-five years this town has been Skillings's muse, his mooring, the setting and subject of most of his fiction. He is a writer for whom place is character and vice versa. His steadfast devotion to his landscape and its inhabitants yields depth of vision, shades of variety. Provincetown is the Copernican sun around which, for this writer, all else revolves.

His work ranges from the very short story to the novel, in addition to poetry. His first collection of stories, *Alternative Lives*, was published in 1974, followed by *P-town Stories (or The Meat-rack)* in 1980, *In a Murderous Time* in 1984, and *Where the Time Goes* in 1999. A novel, *How Many Die*, and a novella, *Obsidian*, appeared in 2001. A collection of poems, *Memory for Marisa Rose*, was published in 2003.

The present collection of stories, his eighth book, maps the journey of the writer's life: childhood and upbringing in Bath, Maine; post-collegiate years spent in Boston; and the discovery and subsequent adoption of Provincetown. As such, it is a portrait in three acts of New England itself, from its shipyards and summer camps, to its mixed-race urban neighborhoods of the 1960s, to what arguably remains its most unconventional outpost. It is a portrait of the region's evolution, its gentrification and, in certain respects, its decline. It is a polyphonic portrait of rich and poor, WASPs and minorities, men and women, young and old.

The stories set in Maine are layered ruminations on innocence and loss. Skillings's young characters thirst for experience, for elsewhere. They are sensitive, solitary boys, almost always aware of their "small knowledge of life." They pass idyllic summers idle, flattening pennies on train tracks. The young narrator of "The Rights of Salvage" thinks of his parents as ancestors, his home a confining museum.

I chafed to escape to my favorite playground, the old shipyards, where we hopped from piling to piling or with arms outstretched walked the rotted timbers of sagging wharves. . . . Only a faint clangor reached us from the iron works a mile downriver, and I dreamed of far places, the East Indies perhaps or the Cape of Good Hope.

While the young yearn for escape, and for experience, the old, "dazed by the thought of everything vanishing," long to be young again. They revisit the past, estranged by it, still struggling to decipher it. Some, for whom memory falters, dream simply of remembering.

The Boston stories are located in the city's South End. We move from Maine's dark glassy lakes and loon calls to a gritty landscape of nightclubs, STD clinics, and funeral parlors. Many of the protagonists make a conscious choice to live apart from their families, to forge a separate path. They reject what they come from and gravitate toward the unknown. Two of these stories are love stories, unlikely interracial couplings that would have been considered controversial at the time.

"The Blue Stone," a moving portrait of the artist as a young man, explores the hard choice and practice of living by and for one's writing.

I set out to paper my room with rejections. The size of a wall, the small-ness of a slip—even the most elegant, embossed and tinted—in time dulled the romance of failure, and one glum day, when I got six stories back in the same mail, I forswore the ceremonial bonfire I had planned for them, and dropped them in the trash. That night I caught a glimpse of myself in the window—a rich man's decadent son killing time.

Every artist, at some point, has felt the futility of his or her contribution, and at the same time the necessity of it. Skillings does not flinch from self-examination, devastating as it may be.

In addition to recounting one writer's beginnings, "The Blue Stone," like most of the stories set in Boston, is an affecting exploration of the racial politics that marked the city at the time. Skillings discreetly evokes the bigotry that hangs in the air as the Racial Integration Act of 1965 requires forced busing in Boston, as violence erupts and protests rage. His characters embrace idealism and yet instinctively apprehend its limits. Rick, the protagonist of "What Befell Her," enamored of a black dancer, harbors "a constant, cloudy daydream of them uniting for a better world, but he could never tell her this for fear she would think him naive."

In Provincetown we encounter more aspiring writers, working-class locals, draft-dodgers, Vietnam vets. We find ourselves at an all-night party, in a nursing home, in various bars. One story has as its characters Fellows at the Fine Arts Work Center, which, in addition to his fiction, has been one of Roger Skillings's great contributions to the world. He has been an integral part of its growth, serving as trustee and chair of its writing committee for twenty years. His tireless, boundless faith in young writers has changed the destinies of many, including my own. Those who know Skillings admire his dedication to others. Those who come to this collection as a means of introduction will perceive his dedication to his art.

His fiction reflects a lifetime of brave artistic soldiering, of following no fashion or trend. He honors his literary forebearers without affect. He lives and works from the edges, knowing instinctively that this is the writer's place. As a result his work remains untouched by conventional currents, commonplace themes.

These are ripe, rueful tales, crepuscular in spirit and yet urgent, at times blazing with romance, with desperation. A young man, infatuated with a woman he has just spent the night with but barely knows, wants to buy a red ribbon for her hair. A woman craving sex pulls down her stretch pants in a bar, exposing herself. His technique suggests plein-air painting: a writer in the field, observing, absorbing, and sure-handedly capturing what he sees and hears. He is a master of dialogue, knowing how people speak in bars, in barbershops, at parties. He marries his own voice to those of others, always faithfully. Though elemental and at times astringent, his stories are characterized by wit and warmth. He is a writer who delights in humankind and at the same time despairs of it. He understands the plight of those who have no one to call their own.

Death looms in these tales, accidental, intentional, inevitable. Some die alone, dimly recalled. But places also die, leaving us equally bereft. Small towns in Maine turn into shopping malls, the hardscrabble bars of Provincetown are replaced by upscale restaurants and shops. Boston's South End, as it is described in this book, scarcely exists today. Skillings describes the emotional impact of that change, the brutality of it.

Art is what does not shift or erode, what outlives us, what accompanies us from beginning to end. The following line in "The Rights of Salvage," describing the fingerprinting of a group of fifth-grade boys who have been caught stealing iron, perhaps alludes to this idea: "Our unique whorls would follow us through life, and nothing we did wrong would remain unknown or ever be forgotten." Self-expression identifies the artist, tethering him to the world. If all art is a form of doing wrong, a breaking of the rules, then the same could be said of the work of Roger Skillings—unique whorls that mark both these pages and the reader, stories that will not go unknown, or be forgotten.

— *Jhumpa Lahiri*

The Rights of Salvage

◇◇◇◇◇◇◇◇◇◇◇◇◇◇◇◇◇◇

As kids we was always just dubbin' around—or doin' nothin'—a distinction unclear to adults and now, so many years later, dim even to me. Once we almost set the old shipyards on fire, when the fluffy stuffings of a mattress we'd ripped open and sprayed with lighter fluid blazed up in a raging, towering inferno, igniting the overarching trees, surpassing our most gleeful apprehensions. By the time a fire truck came we were scared out of our wits, watching the fall leaves flare and dance on the wind off the river, snowing ashes on the bramble-covered foundations and rotted pilings.

"What you little shavers up to?"

"Nothin'."

"What d'you mean nothin'?"

"Just dubbin' around."

"With matches? Get home."

At first there were four of us in our secret club, then five, counting Arty, the littlest, who was chubby and unable to keep up, though stolid when bullied or ignored. We'd let him in only because Luke, the next youngest, had showed him where our hideout was. Luke still didn't inhale, but Arty refused to smoke at all, or even throw rocks at the glass insulators on the telephone poles beneath the wooden bridge over the railroad tracks on Oak Street.

He was game but too small to see over the board fence the time we rolled the biggest snowball we could lift, balanced it on top of the railing, then at just the right moment let it drop down the chuffing smokestack of a slow freight. It shot back up instantly on a fountain of hot smoke, hung majestic and sooty before our smarting blinks, then fell without effect into the black, diminishing din.

We argued over what it would take to derail a train, flattened many a penny to the thinness of skin.

We, the first five, including Jimmy, whose father was stationed in Germany, were blood brothers, having touched wrists all around in unspoken vows, till Ritto snatched my jackknife.

"It don't count if we don't draw blood," he said.

"It's symbolic," I said. "You don't really have to do it."

"It won't hurt, you're just chicken," he said, and sawed at his flesh.

A line of red welled in the white cut, but the rest of us refused to try it, and eventually pressed our wrists to his, sharing the nearly impalpable smear, each with each. His sisters we hardly knew by name, as if they belonged to a different tribe. Ritto was the toughest of us, being poorest and most daring. Short, muscular, and grimy, sixth of nine kids, he was always getting kept back in school, so no one ever quite knew his age. His brothers had gone to reform school or God knows where. One or another of these roughnecks was always after us till Ritto's accession by our timorous gang made them protectors instead of dread ambushers, and the way to and from school ceased to be a gauntlet.

In his world fights were the rule, starting with family snarls, progressing from wrestling to fists in their dirt yard, then rocks, slingshots and BB guns at long range, finally even .22s in the woods, prizing to shower some bark on a hiding place. His father had drowned on a bet trying to swim the river drunk between tides; his mother was a hoarse, hard-smoking harridan with wild white hair, knocked-out teeth, and a shriek answerable only by her lipsticked, scrawny daughters in whom we were too young to take interest.

A late only child, I hated to stay home among the antiques. In the silent, dusky house my parents seemed more like ancestors, and I chafed to escape to my favorite playground, the old shipyards, where we hopped from piling to piling or with arms outstretched walked the rotted timbers of the sagging wharves, which every spring were found to have lost whole sections. On hot cloudy afternoons the water was tepid and dragonflies with blurred wings swayed near our heads. We sat and dangled our legs, eager for the next treasure or mysterious cargo of the tides, undid bags of dead kittens and rocks, were baffled, bothered by milky, white balloons. Only a faint clangor reached us from the iron works a mile and a half downriver, and I dreamed of far places, the East Indies perhaps or the Cape of Good Hope, words, not yet even locations on maps to me.

I did not care to realize that the clipper ship had ceased to exist, even in living memory. The stern-faced, cigar-champing stranger in the photographs in the upstairs hall, my paternal grandfather, was born aboard his own father's square-rigger in Calcutta, had carried brass knuckles, brushed his teeth with whiskey, and, having held place well into the era of steam and steel, had retired from command of the *S.S. Cristobal*, flagship of the Panama Line, built a cottage within sight, but beyond sound, of the all-demanding sea—then died before he ever slept a single, silent summer night in it.

Ship paintings and saturnine portraits of ministers hung on every wall of my parents' house, half a dozen sea chests lay eerily empty in the attic, the library lamps had come from China, and the mantle displayed a cigar cutter made of an exploded shell from the battle-ship *Maine*.

Nowadays the only vessel that berthed in the reach was an orange collier from Norfolk, but the grandeur of the vanished sail entranced me, and in the grocery store, trailing my mother, I looked askance at the absorbed shoppers who showed no signs of regret at the outcome of their history.

My father, the realist, tried to damp down these fancies. In an essay for school I described the decaying yards and an ancient schooner wrecked on the rocks. Perusing my pages, he made inquiry, and hearing that it was really a mud-bound scow slippery with gull slime, observed that it could therefore be neither ancient nor a schooner, nor were there any rocks along that stretch of the river.

A scow, I wanted to say, would spoil my picture, but his principles were unassailable, and when he was safely re-engrossed in the newspaper, I mimed some erasures and changes, and went to bed that night with a sense of self-vindication.

Exercising an unchallenged right of salvage, our club began to glimpse the possibilities of industry, commerce, and wealth. The riverfront was an inexhaustible source of rusty nuts, bolts, bars, spikes, and the like that we collected by the cartload, for which Jedlo the junk dealer paid us a penny a pound. We meant to build a clubhouse, with real windows and a door that could be padlocked. Thus we slogged in the mudflats, pried bolts out of beams, speeding the dissolution of our domain, came home filthy, left our clothes in the cellar, were elated to find that in less than a month we had saved ten dollars.

One hot day, hauling a load of scrap down an alley to Jedlo's, we noticed the open back door of Lovell's Laundry. In a sort of cobwebbed storage room four rusty gears were piled in a corner. We could hear the rhythmic thumping of oiled machinery.

"Fifty pounds apiece I'll bet," Ritto said. "We oughta heist one."

"We better not, we'll get caught," Luke said.

"We won't get caught," I said.

"What'll we do if we do?" Jimmy said.

"Play it by ear," Rit said.

I admired his favorite expression, as I did his scorn of fear. He was a constant truant, always in flight from punishment for infractions it would not have occurred to any of us to wish to commit, and he was brave. He was scratched and bruised from flying through the air and sometimes falling, trying impossible feats in our network of ropes hung from trees high over the embankment, but he always sprang up fierce against pain, ready to try again. He had been born a bad boy, and my grandmother always said, "He'll come to grief some day, sure as fate."

We helped him heave one of the gears onto the cart, and then in a contagion of panic began running it full-tilt over the cobblestones, the cart spewing bits of iron as it jounced on its wobbly wheels. "Slow down," Ritto hissed. "Act natural."

At the junkyard Jedlo came out of his shed. Unshaven, with a smudged forehead, gray unruly hair, sad eyes, and a suit as wrinkled and dirty as any workman's clothes, he handled trainloads of scrap on contract as well as petty business like ours, and he was pallid, as if the sun never touched him. Once I peeped in the window before he heard us and saw him sitting on a bare cot, with his head in his hands, elbows propped on his knees.

As usual we put our junk on the scale and he adjusted the weights.

"Where'd that come from?" he said.

"Where'd what come from?" Ritto said.

"That," Jedlo said.

"What?" Ritto said.

"Looks like from the laundry," Jedlo said.

"Naw," Ritto said. "We get all our stuff from the yards."

"Dollar seventy-two," Jedlo said.

Ritto skipped around him, peered up at the scale. "Dollar seventy-three," he said.

"Okay, boys, dollar seventy-three," the junk dealer said, fishing from a vast pant pocket a ball of bills and a spill of coins. "Throw your stuff on the pile, and dump that around in back."

The pile was a hill of every conceivable kind of scrap, chopped, mangled, shredded, and cracked. Copper and lead were like gold at twenty cents a pound and made their own little mounds, but could seldom be found anywhere, and never an ounce in the old yards.

Now discord entered our affairs. We went on scavenging, but only Arty's exuberance remained. We elders with muddy clothes and cut fingers felt how hard, futile, even foolish such toil was, and one day, without quite voicing our intentions, we nervously trundled half a cartload of iron and a burlap bag down the alley, and swiped a second gear.

An hour later with wary eyes we took the last two to Jedlo, who bought them without comment.

His wordless, unblinking complicity struck me as sinister, but I knew he was a Jew, which seemed to explain. He had built a new house, my father said, but his wife refused to move in, so no one lived there, though the lawn was mowed and the shrubbery pruned, year after year.

"I hope he don't tell on us," Luke said.

"He knew right where they came from," I said.

"Play it by ear," Ritto said. "Only the cops care, and they're paid to."

He spoke with bitter spite, his whole family having been plagued by these meddlesome men in humiliating blue, who kept implacably knocking on their door in pursuit of one member or another, and never seemed ready to leave them alone.

It was not long after our entry into theft, and the consequent changes wrought in our views, that a kid named Oz moved into the vacant Victorian house on Grove Street. Its tall peak could be seen from Luke's low front porch. We let Oz follow us around for a couple of hours one day, then trailed into his newly fenced backyard, where a croquet course and a badminton net had been set up.

Ritto jeered at the sissy games, kicked a wicket sky-high, and then whacked a croquet ball with a flimsy little racket, which broke. He snorted, snatched another, tossed the wooden ball up again.

Oz slapped him in mid-swing. Ritto dropped the racket and slammed Oz in the chest with the heels of his hands. His balance regained, Oz not very happily pushed back at the much smaller vandal, who with easy contempt slammed him again with both hands.

Oz's mother came out. Her first words told us she was different from anyone we had ever known, stranger by far than her son, who was merely more polite than we were, more mature. Her husband was a planning consultant, one of the influx that brought Urban Renewal and the schemes of the fifties that transformed the outskirts of small towns into malls, the business districts into vacant stores and ghostly vistas.

I could see through one uncurtained window of their living room and out another to a wide view of the river. They seemed to have many mirrors and no furniture. Ritto's small, asphalt-shingled house

I had never been in, beyond the mudroom, with its pungent smell of old poverty—torn tar paper, charred linoleum, kerosene, ashes, cats, and unwashed clothes—airless, dingy, dim.

At Luke's I was sometimes fed a peanut-butter-and-marshmallow-fluff sandwich, which seemed the main fare in that fatherless house of six children, who were always neatly dressed in old hand-me-downs. On Fridays Luke preferred to fast than to eat fish. Once his high school English-teacher mother turned him over her knee when she caught him in those two sustaining jars. I never forgot the blank stare she cast upon my discomfited Protestant swallowings.

George's father was a swashbuckling plumber who loved to swear in front of us and boast about charging the daylights out of his dimwit customers, besting them at deals, or making off with radiators or rare fixtures more valuable than the fancy new ones he persuaded them to have him install. He would describe with sly gusto the provocative women he had to fend off on his jobs, squint at us through the smoke of his Lucky Strike, and declare, "By the Goddamned Jesus, she had a set of jugs the size of watermelons."

Then he would cough loudly, masterfully hawk a lunger, and spit the grey clot over the porch railing with amazing velocity and reach. Luke's mother wore a permanent face of resigned disapproval, made grotesque when she couldn't help laughing; she was the sternest disciplinarian of all our mothers, never hesitating to treat us as hers. My mother addressed us all alike, as adults with customs slightly curious but tolerable.

Arty the prudent, with three older sisters, came from a family of feminine piety. Pastel pictures of a dreamy Jesus adorned every room. Arty's father was a burly-bellied fireman who drank whiskey in silence till his face shone red, but seldom spoke, except to second his wife, and never twice, his mild volume exerting total authority. He called balls and strikes all over the county, and was famous for having ejected an infield umpire who refused to be overruled by him on a play at third base.

Arty's mother was a wisp with folded arms who ran the house with a whisper, and within her ken no one ever misbehaved, not even Ritto.

Said Oz's cosmopolitan mother in accents jaunty and brisk, "If you're going to fight you may as well do it right." While we stood around cockeyed, she drew a square ring in the dirt driveway with a stick and prepared to referee. The biggest of us all, Oz didn't want to fight, but looked doomed to do as told. We others waited between gloating and gloom, dreading fights ourselves.

"Shake hands," she said. "Fight fair."

Ritto blew on his grime-engraven knuckles and walloped Oz on the nose. Blood ran down and dripped from his chin in large, glistening drops.

"No hitting in the face," wailed the amazed matron, younger by ten years than any of our mothers. She hugged her silent son's head to her white silk blouse, but I caught a glimpse of his steady eyes and later wondered what would have happened had she not been there to intervene.

We were relieved to be asked to leave and went off to indulge in braggadocio and triumph over alien interlopers. No more did we sail rafts or net minnows in tide pools or angle for eels. We still met at our hideout, a pine-needle nest amid a palisade of trees, and smoked a cigarette before setting out for downtown and its back alleys, but now our motives had sharpened. We savored our new sense of outlawry, and our eyes as we walked darted everywhere.

Beyond the bridge, for a mile along the river, impregnably fenced, monstrous and inimical to romance, with its echoing staccato of riveting and white flashes of acetylene, stretched the ways and sheds of the iron works, which had launched more destroyers than the entire Japanese Empire in the Second World War, and was still going full blast, erecting the hulls of guided-missile frigates, eventually for the West Germans, one such ship christened the *Erwin Rommel*.

This phantasmagoric machine world gave me bad dreams and seemed to mock the remnants of the old wharves whence had sailed the legendary clipper ship. These modern bows soared above the neighboring roofs, and the cranes that swung the steel plates into place ran on wheels that would have crushed a horse. Inside that high, unclimbable chain-link fence with barbed wire strung outward along the top was scrap metal enough for a zillion clubhouses, but we never gave it a thought.

Nor did the civilian town provide. The four laundry gears proved to be a bonanza never matched. We found no more open doors, and weeks passed in futile search while our impatience and ruthlessness grew and we took to letting air out of tires and ripping doors off garbage bins. We loved to break things, cast-iron pipes with a hammer, anything fragile, all glass. Windows abandoned to spiders were impossible to resist—then came flight, with its thrill of fear and the relief of distance and safety.

Once, when we were wreaking havoc, Mr. Cohen the clothier came out of his store's back door in a gray sweater and old flannels—not far from my father's office—and spoke to us with open palms in beautiful accents so kindly and reasonably that we were astounded, and went off strangely ashamed, ceased our depredations entirely for several days, and thereafter took care never to attract his notice again.

Many years later, soon after my father died, I caught a last glimpse of him, very old and frail looking. He seemed to be trying to dance toward me, his hands aflutter, half-held back by uncertainty. I felt puppet strings pulling me to recognize him and speak, but the moment failed of shyness, and he went from sight; it grieves me still.

The clubhouse we would build would be a mansion, a palace, a castle, a fort. *Citadel* was the word we vied for but never found. The more we planned, the grander our wants, the greater the possibilities appeared, and pure schemes seemed future certainties. We must have known winter gales would batter down any walls we could ever build on any wharf, yet we never tried to envisage our clubhouse anywhere except on the very end of the longest wharf still standing, and it doomed by the next hard storm.

Walter Gage's Auto Body Shop stood on low pilings at the top of a steep embankment. Its roll-up doors faced Water Street, on a higher level, but in back its red, corrugated tin wall had neither door nor windows. Six feet below, where an empty lot grew Queen Anne's lace, thistles, buttercups, dandelions, devil's paintbrush, purple vetch, rhubarb, and burdocks, the sidewalk had buckled and split and nearly disappeared in the general neglect. Men drank there at all hours from pint bottles of liquor and wine that we broke with rocks and our baseball arms.

One day the dark cavern under the garage caught our eyes: we had never been in there, we who went everywhere unimpeded, over fences, across roofs, through gardens and yards.

Ritto climbed the embankment, crawled between two pilings, after a moment whistled, and we followed him up and in.

In the twilight a mound of metal refuse rose beneath the trapdoor above.

"Thousands of stuff," Arty breathed.

We squatted on our heels and looked at the formidable pile, weighing the risks of what might be found in the silent garage overhead.

"Come on," Arty said, and for once he led.

Reluctantly, in a growing frenzy of frustration, we half-filled our burlap bag and dragged it down the embankment with cut fingers, irritated to think how few pennies would result. We were just trying to spew the awkward load through the bag's limp mouth when a patrol car bumped up over the sidewalk and whirred its siren once.

"Keep right on," Ritto said sidelong. He finished emptying the bag, then scrambled up the embankment with it. "Come on!" he yelled, but we were rooted.

Two policemen got out of the car stiffly and slowly, slammed both doors with one sound, and strolled toward us, looking leisurely about as if we were not the only objects of their interest.

"All right, boys, what've you got there?" said the older one.

"Nothing much," Luke finally said, having ventured an upward glance and been caught by the asker's eye.

"Nothing?" he asked gravely.

"Just scrap iron," Luke amended.

Arty stood like a snowman, eyes and mouth wide open.

"Hey, you, come outta there. Come on now," the young cop yelled at the invisible Ritto.

I feared he might try to hide or climb through the trapdoor, but after a hair-raising delay he appeared dragging the cumbersome bag, face red with exertion and choler. He stumbled coming down the embankment, but the young cop caught his arm and kept him from falling.

"Well, what've we got here?" the old cop said jovially.

We looked at the cartload of rusted rubble. The cops looked at us.

"Scrap iron, eh?"

"Yes sir," said Luke.

"Now you fellas know better than that," the old cop said. "Don't you now?"

"Yes sir," Luke said, scuffing the gravel.

"Do you know what you were doing?" The old one ruffled Arty's hair. "Huh? Come on now, what were you doing?"

"Stealing," Arty said in a sepulchral voice.

"We just didn't think," Luke said.

"Sure," the old one said. "I got a kid your age." He glanced at his impassive partner. "Now I know you fellas didn't mean any harm, so we'll let it go this time. You put that iron back where you found it and we'll forget all about it. Fair enough?"

"Yes sir," Luke said, including us all in his nod, and let out a long held breath. Arthur finally closed his mouth; Ritto kicked a rock; my face burned.

"Okay, boys," the young one concurred, and they turned toward the car.

"We wasn't stealing," Ritto said almost to himself with matter-of-fact disdain.

The cops' momentum carried them on another step before they stopped and turned back.

"Then what in hell were you doing?" the young one said.

"Now listen," said the old one quietly, "you were taking iron that belongs to someone else. That's stealing. I been pretty square with you fellas and I don't want any backtalk."

"That iron don't belong to nobody," Ritto said. "It's just junk Mr. Gage drops through the floor to get rid of it."

"Aw, Rit, don't make it any worse," Luke said.

"What d'you think this is, a debate?" the old cop said, resting his hands on his belt-bulged hips, forehead starting to sweat in the sun.

"I don't know nothin' about them," Ritto averred in that same flat, fatal, matter-of-fact voice, "but I wasn't stealing nothin.'"

The ominously lengthening silence made me want to run, but where I didn't know, for we had all been fingerprinted in the seventh grade. A vexed policeman had rolled our fingers on the pad, then on our cards, and explained that our unique whorls would follow us through life, and nothing we did wrong would remain unknown or could ever be forgotten.

"Well, well," said the old one at last in a steely tone, "we have a difference of opinion." His eyes came around to me. "What about you? You act like you're not even here."

I had been trying to disappear by keeping perfectly still and staring so intently into space that my eyes registered nothing. The others had edged off toward Arty, whose mouth was gaping again. Ritto stood by himself.

"We wasn't stealing nothin,'" he said again, precluding any mediation I might have tried.

"Get in the car," the old one snapped at him, all friendliness gone.

"You others put that iron back where you found it, and get home."

We four began to shuffle and fumble with the cart and burlap sack. Ritto made for the car with such alacrity I was scared he would drive off in it himself.

The old cop promised, "Him and us, we're going to take a little ride down to the station and we'll either get him straightened out ... or ... or...."

"Know the reason why," the younger supplied over his shoulder as he half-ran with long strides to overtake Ritto and open the back door for him like a chauffeur.

The old one gave us a last glower, ruffled Arty's hair once more, and then followed his partner.

The doors thumped shut upon them and the car rolled slowly, ominously off across the glass-strewn gravel with the maverick's small round head positioned exactly in the middle between the two hexagonal blue caps.

The moment they were out of sight, without a word of dissent, even from Arty, we dumped the cart where it was, leaving a hardly discernible scattering of metal scraps, the last we ever collected.

We went home quick—apprehensive, ashamed of ourselves, amazed at Ritto's folly—and waited for the phone to ring, our parents' questioning to begin. We wasn't doin' nothin', or, if pressed, Just dubbin' around.

Of course Ritto's mother got the only call. She went down to the station, made apologies and promises, and when she got him home gave him a desperate thrashing.

His ascendancy over us briefly increased, but soon our adherence failed and our lives diverged. The dream of the clubhouse remained, but henceforth we earned and saved money separately, mowing lawns and shoveling snow, endeavors he disdained. He had told the truth regardless and paid for it, which fed his furious pride, but it ended our childhood. The merely make-believe to us had always been real to him, and he never deviated from the path of obstinate bravado that led to his early undoing.

Once at Summer Camp

<><><><><><><><><><><><><><><><><><>

Many years ago, when I was a mere Big Brother, not yet even a Junior Counselor training for a paid Counselor's job in some future year, one of my charges caught a gargantuan fish, bigger than I had ever seen or could imagine outside of an ocean.

This was on Damariscotta Lake in Maine. I might have been fourteen. I had a rowboat full of Rabbits, one in the bow, two on the next seat—me in the middle with the oars, would-be Uncle Thinks-He's-Big of the Bears—and three more squeezed into the stern.

They all had poles and reels and tackle boxes spilling spools of leader and line, floats, flies, silver spinners, spoons, sinkers, bubbles, jitterbugs, jigs, tangles of worms, dead minnows, baby frogs.

I rowed slowly so they could troll, each with his favored lure or bait, for the finical, flipping little perch or the diabolic bass or patient pickerel. I didn't care a fig for fish. All I loved were games of ball, or a canoe and solitude.

Had Archie, the excited tyke, ever hooked a fish before? Maybe in a dream.

He was actually only a Squirrel, the youngest, smallest of them all. He whispered at first nibble, bewailed the slack that followed on, shrilled at the strike, while the rest yelled, "Yeah!" at the visible pull, the taut line pleating the placid surface.

He reeled and held, grimaced, scrunched, squeaked with panic and strain, keeping the pole-butt stuck under his belt.

The others yelled unceasing advice, squirming as if they had to pee, yanking their own lines every two seconds till they forgot them as Archie's pole bent double and our triumphal din rang across the water.

I shipped oars to help and felt a steady, stolid drag like a dead log. When the fish emerged, motionless, no fight in it, we hauled it over the side in silent wonderment, let it fall with an awful flop and lie there untouched, gills gaping, one inscrutable eye fixed on us or the sky, the other flush on the floorboards of that bulky, balky scow of a flat-bottomed boat that had no keel and wouldn't row straight, couldn't have capsized in a gale even if we had all sat on one gunwale, and in the least breeze would sail right onto the rocks or out to sea, so to speak, whereat pallid Uncle Zeke the vigilant would chug to the rescue with his chagrining Evinrude.

That was one venerable fish, out of time, out of place, weak with age, wise to fate, never measured, never weighed, never to be wholly apprehended.

The crowding Rabbits craned and crowed, "Way to go, Archie, way to go."

"We'll feast," said I, "for a week," but they looked squeamish. It was much too hoary to eat.

"We'll get it stuffed," I tried, "and mounted on a plaque with all our names and hang it in the Lodge."

This won a unanimous cheer. The Lodge—where mornings began with a Thought for the Day and evenings ended with a hymn and a prayer before Lights Out and Taps—was a pine-slab place of plain benches, flying squirrels in the rafters, a stage for skits and stunts, and a Cyclopean, glacial-boulder fireplace built by the first campers, above which hung a portrait of the Chief's son, who had died of blood poisoning at twenty-nine from a neglected blister on the heel, and who on his birthday every year was eulogized as an example of probity and service.

I would sit and stare at his clear face while the camp sang "I Would Be True."

The Chief was the founder of Wavus Camps and looked like a real Indian in his headdress at Council Fire. He was a self-made educator, missionary in his own world, revered by all, tireless, bronze-weathered, smallish, seventy-five, with straight black hair, callused hands, gold-tipped lower front teeth, and a visage more greatly graven than Uncle Stan's or Uncle Evan's or even Uncle Zeke's. When he spoke, all listened, all adopted his mild, versatile American Christianity of character, high ideals, unselfishness, effort, devotion, and humility, blended with lessons of how to live in the woods, after the manner of the Indians, our haunting predecessors, who held all nature holy.

Well, that fish was truly prodigious, worthy indeed to be hung in the Lodge among other immortal if smaller catches, but in fact it was spawned for no trophy.

It was the primeval hour of evening when the orange sun, half down the western shore, arcs unearthly large, close and portentous; nothing stirs lake surface or air; midges stop wings without falling; all motion ends and solid silence holds a stillness so whole it might have seemed eternal but for the commotion of our fish-catching and the boatload of Cayugas rowed near by Aunt Helen.

Cayugas were girls the age of Rabbits. They lived in their cluster of cabins named after Native American tribes in the pines at the foot of the drumlin climbed by our progress of animal signs: Squirrels, Rabbits, Foxes, Beavers, and Bears, ending at the top with Stags, Buffaloes, and Elephants.

We had the sun, stars, and flagpole, wind-rung by brass bolt-snaps; we saw the wheeling hawks, knew the exuberance of running barefoot, full tilt, downhill in the dark, next thing to flying.

They walked the soft, pine-needle paths, had the shady rock-bound lakeshore, chipmunks, lichens, ferns. All heard eerie owl and loon.

This was Aunt Helen's first and only year, the only year of her husband, Uncle Alton of the Stags. They hadn't been married long and in public nudged and kept closer together than the other middle-aged couples accustomed to separate cabins. Nearly twice her age, he showed a grizzled mien when he skipped a shave; she was golden, shy, defiant of her beauty.

By July's end something had gone wrong. Through an opening in the trees I could see from my top bunk during Rest Periods, while I read *Around the World in Eighty Days*, how she would stand behind her screen door and refuse to let him in. Much my favorite counselor, he now grew irascible with me—baleful for no reason—whom he had favored in the first weeks of summer.

I began to shun him, drop my gaze before his strange glare, amazed to feel the glamour of coach and former baseball star fade into fear, while my allegiance switched to our Bears' own mundane Uncle Satch the clown—no athlete—who, otherwise a dignified college man, would light a match to his farts in the dark and squeal with high glee as we marveled giddily at the crepitating blue flame.

"Keep your underpants on," he cautioned, "or you'll get singed." But we dared not try it, and after Taps would importune, especially on Saturday nights following our feast of homemade brown bread, coleslaw, and baked beans.

What the Chief would have said I can't conceive. I guess he might have been bemused by the sight of Uncle Satch on his back on his bunk holding his knees with one hand, trying to position the perilous, short-lived match with the other, red-faced, gasping as he conjured a wind to surpass all past prodigies, though such antics must have seemed excess to Uncle Percy, Tennis Counselor Emeritus, for whom subtlety, not force, should tell.

I wanted to smash the ball straight through the court to China, but he—suave, always smiling in fresh white ducks, white shirt, bow tie, floppy white hat with celluloid green eyeshade on his almost bald head, face deeply lined, deeply tanned—would make us guard the net, not swing, only slant the racquet's plane decisively against the sharp shots he whacked at us.

Not forever to neglect our long-suffering fish, nor stretch theme, I'll simply recapitulate that it was a whopper—and only add that it was all the more monumental a victory for me personally because of an odd occurrence in the very afternoon before that orange-tinged evening of the tyro Archie's approach to early apotheosis, when, down at the lake for our weekly bath, naked among the Bears, each with washcloth and bar of soap, I got to swearing out of control.

I Goddamned this and I Goddamned that—the dive I botched, the sharp rock underfoot, the confusion perhaps of all my thoughts. Once started, I couldn't stop. Every few seconds I had to swear.

Uncle Zeke said, "Hey!"

"God damn it!" I replied to myself, but loud.

"Hey!" said Uncle Zeke, Head Counselor and the Chief's right hand.

Everyone respected his grave, rueful ways, good humor, and wry, kind eye. He had ulcers, I now surmise from the medicines he kept on his shelf, though I never heard him complain.

But not one minute could I keep quiet. "Goddamn Jesus Christ!" I said next, to my maddened bewilderment.

Zeke took a quick look at me. "Enough!" said he.

I didn't want to swear again, but when I opened my mouth, out came an oath, nor could I recant. My cabinmates were gaping, lathering themselves with suds, swimming underwater to rinse, bursting up to clear eyes and ears and hear another resounding Goddamn! I was terrorized myself.

Uncle Zeke, heretofore imperturbable on all known occasions, turned his whole torso, flabby breasts and white belly, where he sat astride the great Saddle Rock, and took me in with a bleak gaze ever more detached, unfamiliar, and hard, as if he had never really surveyed me before and now didn't like what he saw.

What I meant that day so long ago I can't say, but what I said was, "Goddamn!" and then I had to "Goddamn!" again in pure, amazed chagrin.

I had always been a good camper, always got my Social Point, the jewel, a little brass stud the Chief stamped on our leather wrist straps at Monday Assembly, signifying that the possessor had passed moral muster for the week.

I realized I would lose my first one here this very day, and wouldn't care, would never care for such things again.

Then something further entered Uncle Zeke's eyes, some minatory sign of imminent release, which didn't so much frighten as give me over to a pity new to my small knowledge of life. I knew he could silence me if he had a mind to, even if it wasn't exactly me. I saw he could have no choice and I clenched my teeth and finally shut up, but what disturbed me most was the realization that I could speak or keep silent, but if I spoke I must curse.

Zeke may have thought it strange, but then he was used to boys. He never mentioned it again. I had no further visits of profanity, and the episode passed into oblivion, though that effing fish has surfaced persistently through the years from my ever-uneasy depths.

Fantastically big that fish was, and all hands, even if they were only cubs—and Archie in particular—understood perfectly well what a prodigious feat catching it had been.

Aunt Helen, enclosed in her golden glow, with little dripping oar dips drew near in a sweet-ribbed, round-bottomed, easily maneuvered boat, and all her crew of Cayugas yelled to know what our ruckus was about.

No one was equal to telling them, nor to quelling their scoffing, and finally I hoisted the fish high, as proudly as if I'd caught it myself. I felt vindicated of my swearing fit, and redeemed, my charges all ecstatic and undrowned.

There it hung, beneath my two straining hands, for an instant, in all its still immensity, with its great, bulging, cloudy eyes; then it gave a ferocious flip, slipped the hook, plunged, and vanished with hardly a splash, leaving a fading silver flash and a few ripples.

Archie watched the water regain the solid black of oncoming dusk, then looked at me. The others followed his eyes to mine, read there, heard in my staring silence, the irrevocable truth, and with one voice began to bawl. The girls burst out in giggles.

I remember consternation, my first despair of remorse, a premonition of future complexities, but especially the look Aunt Helen gave me of curiosity, sympathetic reproof, and absolutely naked womanly interest. I had never been looked at like that, and gazed back mesmerized.

She smiled at last vaguely, a little remotely, her eyes skimming each of us, murmured something to her Cayugas, dipped her oars in deft, melodious sculls, and the boat turned like a leaf in an eddy and glided away on the glassy, dark lake.

The moment possessed me, grew long, made all my present follies fade. Rowing slowly toward the dock, I hardly heard my Cubs' laments, saw no hope of atonement, but for many years, even after I had surmounted my virginity, even after I was older than she was then, I dreamt of her with a bright, untarnished innocence.

The next summer, to my vast disappointment, she did not return, neither she nor Uncle Alton, having brought a note of discord in. That last August, I now recall, he slapped one of the Stags, who, being nearly full-grown, slapped him back.

The Tomb of Hiram Gooms

◇◇◇◇◇◇◇◇◇◇◇◇◇◇◇◇◇◇◇◇◇◇◇◇◇

It was hot as blazes that summer, the hottest on record, 1967. I went in the Clipper about ten. I'd already had a few, and there was my cousin Jenny at the bar, shocked me out of a year. She was just seventeen. Of course she thought she was smart as all get-out. She'd got her tight jeans on, no bra, not that she needed one, and the top buttons of her shirt were undone.

The place was full of downriver boys. I'm related to half of them, and they all love to fight. That's their main recreation. Best keep an eye out. I lost a tooth one time, and I wasn't even involved. Bub gave Johnny B. an awful belt, and Johnny jumped up and knocked me cold. He said he was sorry, but he had to laugh.

I came up behind and said in Jenny's ear, "Fancy finding you here."

She gave a squeal and hugged me; the jukebox came on and she started singing. She had—for all I know may still have—a pure country voice. She knew all the words to everything, all that mouse crap about cheating hearts and lonesome blues. It's that wail that always rubbed me wrong, that break in the voice. I used to tell myself, Never mind, tomorrow's another night.

I said, "I didn't know you was so grown up."

She said, "I only drink ginger ale. Billy don't charge me."

Billy the bartender, bald little guy in a white shirt with rolled-up sleeves—dead three years now—never said a word unless he had to. I had him once, but then he pretended it never happened. Maybe he forgot. I don't forget anything, not anymore.

I said, "Jenny, your father'd have a fit."

"Don't worry," she says. "I come alone, I leave alone."

So she says. But that don't last forever. Everybody was milling around and yelling, guys trying to buy her a real drink. She was so innocent, she flirted with everyone, didn't even know she was doing it. I could just see some big brawl a-brewing.

She got out on the dance floor with a nut I knew. Good-looking but a nut. He's calmed down some since. When he got her in a hug, I pulled her off the floor. I said, "I don't mind you having a little fun, but not with the likes of in here."

"Okay," she said. "I don't care. What're you doing here yourself?" I said I was gettin' rowdy, which was all right for me, not her.

She just started up singing again. That's what she did at home, when her ma got after her. She wanted to go on records, and she might have, too, if she hadn't got hitched to the wrong man, or men, I guess.

Nut came over, put his arms around us, head between. "'Lo, Mildred," he says. He knew my name was Millicent, came right off a tombstone out back of his family homestead.

"Hello, Nut," I said, and squeezed his hard ass.

He said, "You're calling me a nut?" And gave me the back of his head for Jenny, so I got a good feel. He didn't even notice.

I said, "All you do is crack up your car and brag about how many beers you drank and how close you came to gettin' killed."

He didn't attend at all and I got another CC and ginger. On my other side an old geezer was wheedling this girl, about Jenny's age. She kept shaking her head no. He kept saying, "Why not?" Finally she got so exasperated she said it right out loud: "'Cause I'm your daughter, Dad." I was already three sheets to the wind, and it was hard to keep track of Jenny. Pretty soon I'd see some guy getting her up against him, and I'd go pull her off the floor.

She didn't mind. She knew I'd get distracted. Next thing she's over by the jukebox or the pinball machines or back on the floor with some crumb.

"Milly," she said, "you worry too much. I'm just getting acquainted." I said, "You don't want to know nobody here." Then she was gone again, and this cute little guy came up. College kid he must have been, clean cut, beach tan, not from work—that's for sure. He'd never had a callus; I'll bet to this day he's never had one yet. I could smell his shave. He was so polite, he said "please" and "thank you" to Billy for his beer.

I had one of my hunches. So I pulled out my stretch pants and showed him my bush.

He was the suave type—some guys would grab a handful or stick their heads in, but he just stepped back and gave me a droll roll of the eye that said he was subtle, not about to have his socks knocked off.

I said, "How'd you like to razzle-dazzle me?"

"Oh," he said, "no, thank you, but I do appreciate the offer."

I said, "Ain't you randy at all?"

He gave this little half laugh—his lips never moved, but his stomach jerked. He had these sharp little ears, and he was friendly, no prude, not nervous, not proud. We got talking about the weather: how, bad as it was, winter was worse.

I used to get rambunctious when I drank. Better laugh than cry was my motto. I liked to make things happen. Where all my woes come from—two boys too big for their britches, gone from the nest, thank God, not that I din't love 'em when they come home to get patched up. Two husbands long gone, and umpteen dim-bulb boyfriends, who made themselves scarce, except once every dog's age. I needed to get a little every while or so or I didn't feel right.

That's no crime. I know some people think it is, but they're not standing in my shoes. What *is* a crime is a mannish woman. I never even noticed till someone said it and I went and looked in the mirror. It's not that I'm big. Some men like an armload, they like the comfort. But that face wasn't me—at least I didn't think it was, back then—like a block of granite grim as those formal photographs in Granny's family album, all black clothes like life's one long funeral, never a smile from one generation to the next. I guess I'm just a throwback, no lady wiles, just my own craggy brows and black eyes, sharp as ice picks. So I had to catch them with my tongue, I had to get them laughing.

I'd forgot all about Jenny. I said, "You wait here. I'll be right back." But I couldn't find her anywhere, even in the loo, and then he was gone, too. I couldn't see either of them—just a sea of heads—and I got that old familiar feeling it wasn't going to be my night again. I should never get my hopes up.

So I had another CC and then a beer to cool down. "Billy," I said, "you old goat, you know what I'd like tonight?"

He raised his chin at me. He was long-suffering, but he always tried to oblige.

I said, "I'd like a pole of a prick with a red head like a pomegranate right up my bazoo. I happen to know you've got a whanger on you would make a heifer howl. What say we go out back like we used to do?"

"Please," he said. "There's ladies present."

I got a good guffaw off 'er that. He turned his eyes half an inch. There was a woman and a girl sort of clinging to the cash register, standing so close together they might have been glued, staring straight ahead at the little window that went brr-zing, seventy-five cents, every beer he rung up.

"Billy," I said, "ol' groaner, remember how you used to do me? Let's take up habits again."

He said out of the side of his mouth, "My sister and niece."

"Oh," I said, "pardon me." I didn't mean to get Billy in Dutch.

Next thing, the cute little guy came back. He made a bow, he stepped right up, casual-like, and I said to myself, What was you worrying about? Everything's going your way.

"Honey-bunch," I said, "buy me a drink."

"With pleasure," he said. His wallet was not so fat as I thought it would be. His beer and my CC plus tip about cleaned him out.

I said, "I like you. You're all right with me. You're intelligent, too. That's a rare thing these days. Especially around here."

"Thank you," he says.

I said, "You couldn't be more welcome. I have some brains myself. I have what you might call second sight. I know certain things. For instance I know you're going to come home with me and be pampered like you've never even dreamed of. I hope you have a car, but we can find a ride. Not here, though."

He looked at me no way at all, and my hopes went up. There are three kinds of men—those who will, those who won't, and those who might, and they're always the best. I said, "Do you have a car?"

He said, "Yes," and after a little wait he said, "actually, I do."

"All right," I said, and slipped off my stool. "You go first and I'll follow in about a minute. I doubt Joel would notice, but he'd be liable to introduce himself, put you through the third degree, just to be funny. He's the guy with all the tattoos, he's a cousin of mine, not to mention Bobby and Gum over there by the door. I'd just as soon not incite their interest either. They like to plague me when they can, 'cause I plague them. It's just a way we have. You can finish your beer."

"I'm sorry," he says, "but I'm afraid I have to go."

"With me," I say.

He smiled, but not at me, not at anything, a little pity smile—I could have killed him for that—and then he started to leave, but I grabbed him by the shirt.

"You're going with me," I said, and something changed in his eyes, and then Jenny was pulling on my arm, yelling, "Milly, Milly!"

I let him loose. I'm also pretty strong, which scares them, too. I really thought we'd hit it off. He stood there brushing his wrinkles, looking at Jenny, and her at him, till their eyes got locked, and I said, "Time to scram, Sam."

He jumped his eyebrows to Jenny, just walked off and out the door—while I looked daggers at his back.

"Oh, Milly," Jenny said, "what's got into you? Who was that?"

"Some fairy," I said, but I felt bad. I should've let her have him. I downed the CC and started on his beer. The room tilted and all the faces along the bar rolled by like dimes. I couldn't see Jenny anymore, and what could I do? Maybe she went after him. I hope she did. And caught him, too, but I never heard. Anyway, she got her life like I got mine.

I went outside and sat on somebody's bumper till the whirlies quit, and then I headed for Mayo's Diner. That was the other place in town, in case you wanted to eat. Long and narrow, one counter, six booths, and who would be there at midnight on a Saturday? I couldn't go by without a look-see—no, no, not me.

And there they were, the old folks, each in his booth. Pasty-faced Gridley Mordridge in his blue suit and red tie, all spruced up like always, with his Panama hat beside him. Whitest thing in the whole town. He never looked up from his gin, year in, year out. He inherited a fleabag hotel that got torn down by Urban Renewal. Nothing ever got built there, it's still just rubble.

Next booth—they hardly ever even spoke to each other—Wally Wizzling was drinking his zillionth Pabst Blue Ribbon, just getting to the stage where he'd wave his arms and shout. He was a railroad man. People said he was scared to death he'd get the signals wrong and cause a wreck, and then his wife died.

Last was Hiram Gooms. Deaf, thick glasses, gruff, never bothered anybody, never had friend nor family, far's I ever could find out. He was watching out the window at the bridge like he was counting car lights, south to Boston, north to Bangor, none coming here.

Sometimes I'd get the shivers that one of those cubbyholes was waiting for me. I sat at the exact middle of the counter all by my lonesome. Dottie and Al the cleanup man always stayed at opposite ends, cash register and kitchen. She was a holy terror, but she didn't look it. Al was from my younger days. He was a bully, but life beat him down.

Hiram came right over, told Dottie, "Give Milly the drink I owe her." I said, "You don't owe me anything."

"Owed you a drink," he said. "I always pay my debts."

I'd sent him a drink one night when he was turning his pockets out for last call. Anybody else would've sat a bit and chewed the fat, but he didn't belong to the human race, or maybe he'd resigned. Or maybe he never got the hang of it. I wish I knew.

Next thing, Al Final came over. "Buy me a drink," he said, "my teeth hurt. Dottie won't give me a drop."

I pushed him my CC and he scoffed at it. I said, "What's wrong with your teeth?"

"They're rotten," he says.

I said, "You better see a dentist," but he just laughed. So I bought him another. Dottie didn't charge me. She could never stand the hangdog in him.

Sometimes she'd get on a jag herself, and then she'd let him drink for free. She let him eat there, too. His whole paycheck went in the till, and when that was gone it was either pour or watch him shake, but she was never that mean.

Al was in awful shape. He couldn't stay still; the flies kept lighting on him. Night flies are the worst: you don't expect them, and then you feel their sticky little feet. They won't leave you alone, no matter how you thrash and swat—they jump like fleas. If they took to the air you'd have a chance, but they're too smart.

When Mayo's closed we hung around out front. Dottie's husband drove up and off she went, beddie-bye for her. Grid and Wally tottered single file all over the sidewalk to the corner and disappeared different ways, same as they did every night, mumbling to themselves.

Me, Al, and Hiram were like three zombies with nowhere to go. It was so hot the birds were squealing in the trees and there was something wrong with the streetlight, one of them new ones. It was buzzing and snapping, I was looking at it, and all of a sudden it got so bright it almost blinded me. I saw this little lightning streak inside the bulb, still as it could be for half a second, then it went pop.

I said, "Did you see that?" but nobody did. It was just darker.

"My teeth are killing me," Al said. "Anybody got a bottle?"

"Hiram does," I said, just to stir things up. I wish to God I never said that. I didn't know if he did or didn't. I just said it to sic him on Hiram for being so stodgy.

"You do?" Al said. "Let me have a drink."

Hiram stood there like he'd gone to sleep. You never could tell how much he heard.

"You got a bottle?" Al shouted in his ear.

"Yup," Hiram said, back on his heels, jingling change in both pockets.

"Give me a drink," Al said. "My Christly teeth are killing me."

Hiram went on looking at the board fence across the street. I never knew if he was dumb or smart, or someway touched. He was just himself, I guess, and no one else.

"Come on, can't you give us a drink?" Al says, half snarl, half whine. I could hear he was about to scream.

"Certainly!" Hiram said, like he was too proud to refuse. He started around the back corner, slow as a dream. Al and I followed. The sweat was pouring off me. Hiram reached half a pint of rum from under the busted steps of the old laundry—shingles ripped off, torn tar paper, smell of cat piss—and put it down his pants pocket. All fixed he was for Sunday.

"Give it here," Al said. "God damn you, my teeth are killing me."

Hiram says, "Hold your hosses," and we had to follow him down to River Street, then up the embankment and out on the railroad bridge, one step at a time on each damn tie. It was murky dark, no moon, no gleam on the rails. The other shore was a blank wall of trees. Even then there was only one train a day, the noon freight.

Finally Hiram got where he wanted to be, and we got sat down. Every once in a while a car went overhead on the upper level, whish, like a whisper. You couldn't see the water, or hear it either—it was weird out there, like being in a cave.

"My favorite place," Hiram says. "Day or night."

I said, "You come out here all the time?" I was surprised—it was like a private resort or a kid's hideout—the one thing I ever knew about him.

He said, "Yup." Not another word.

"Peaceful," I said.

He says, "Yup."

I said, "Must be nice in daylight."

He says, "Yup."

All the while Al was begging for the bottle.

I wouldn't have cared if he'd had to wait till dawn.

Hiram acted like it was some kind of occasion, like he was presiding. Maybe nobody else had ever been out there before and he was letting us in on something. He unscrewed the top with a flourish, held the bottle up like he was making a toast to the stars, if you could see any, then handed it to me. I wet my tongue to be polite. Then Al guzzled it.

"Stop at your share," Hiram said, but Al kept swallowing. I couldn't see but I could hear.

Hiram reached across me and grabbed it back—he hadn't had a drink yet himself—and held it out to me again. Old-fashioned gallantry, I guess, only I sat on my hands. I was set to sit all night and see the river get light, but Al grabbed it and got going again. I can still hear his throat click.

I guess Hiram lost his temper. He lunged across me after it. He was way off balance, and Al just hauled him off my knees with one hand. He never even stopped sucking the bottle.

"Hey!" Hiram said—then splash, never another sound.

I yelled, "Hiram!"

"Shut up," Al said.

Pigeons panicked and flapped. I couldn't see none, but I could feel the wind. "Hiram, Hiram!" I yelled. The sound bounced among the girders and the air beat in my face.

I said, "Which way's the tide running? Can he swim?"

Al says, "What's the difference, you ain't going to jump in."

I said, "He'll drown."

Al says, "So? You better keep your mouth shut."

I yelled, "Hiram, are you all right?"

Al clipped me upside the head. "Sober up," he says.

I said, "We better go for help," but I was drunker than I thought. I wasn't too steady, one step at a time on each damn tie in the dark. Lucky I didn't drink any of Hiram's rum. Al might've pushed me off, too.

It took forever to reach the road. There was no one in sight, no phones. The police station was another half mile, and what could they have done?

"Come on," Al said. "You keep your mouth shut."

When we went by the Clipper there were still loud voices in the parking lot. A bottle smashed and a woman screamed; then came laughter and another bottle. I was terrified Jenny would see me. I was praying Hiram would be back in his booth Monday night, wondering what I'd do if he wasn't, and how I'd get through till then.

Al lived over the Quick Shoe Repair in a room with a mess of a mattress on the floor and a hubcap ashtray by the pillow with a whole overflow of butts and ashes.

I couldn't think what to do. Al was tilting his head back, killing the rum. "Milly, you pig," he said, and pushed me down, pulled my pants off, sneakers and all.

I turned my face away. He finally got it in, drooled a little, rolled off me, and lay on his back. "My goddamned teeth," he said, and heaved a sigh.

I said, "What about Hiram?" but Al was having his moment of sleep. Then he gave a snore and a choke, sat up with both hands over his mouth, and puked a whole lapful of splashes all over me.

That was thirty years ago, and nothing ever stuck to me like that night. All those folks are dead now, except for Jenny who's down in Arkansas with five kids, three from her first husband and two more I don't know where from. I saw her about ten years ago; she said she was still singing in the church down there. She was up for a few days, all by her lonesome—I figured she'd split up again. I didn't ask about the kids.

Mayo's is Aesop's Tables now, with real meals and no booths. The Clipper building's all shops, boutiques and whatnot. I never set foot again in either one.

Strange to say, nothing ever came of that night. I checked the tide when I got home—halfway out, would have been running strong. Monday night I put my head in the door of Mayo's, and there was Dottie and Al, and Gridley and Wally. Same on Tuesday and Wednesday. By week's end I knew Hiram Gooms was riding the Gulf Stream for England, unless he fetched up on some island.

I never knew but that one thing about him. I kept expecting to hear something or see a missing-persons report. I didn't know where he lived or came from, or if he worked or was on disability or lived with somebody or had family or how old he was or was he happy or sad or anything at all. I tried to track him down, but nobody'd ever even heard of him. When I thought about it, though, it turned out I knew a whole lot about other people—everybody else I knew, in fact. I could've told a whole book about any of them.

One by one I pumped the Mayo's crew, like I was the cop on the beat—and none of them could say one word about Hiram Gooms, except he probably just left town. None of them thought it was odd, except Dottie, who said maybe it was a mystery we weren't meant to fathom, which gave me the willies till I decided that was plain poppycock.

Al got surly, and wouldn't even answer me. I could have strangled him with my bare hands, up on his filthy mattress, and got away with it, too, but he was such a miserable wretch, I wouldn't do him the favor. And he was the first to die anyway, froze solid in a blizzard in the parking lot right out back of the Shoe Repair, ploughed under a big solid snowbank, fresh pack of Camels in one hand, new pint of vodka in the other. Two weeks he was gone before anyone knew where.

Till then I'd never been glad to hear somebody'd died. First warm day I walked out on the bridge and tried to guess at Hiram's favorite spot, but it all looked the same out there. I looked around—nobody, nobody, nobody—I cupped my palms, I shouted, "Hiram, I'm sorry," and then the tears come down. First time I cried since I was a kid.

I would've gone to Al's funeral to celebrate, but he got shipped up-country where he came from. Dottie got killed on Witch Spring Hill in a head-on skid. She couldn't stand town water, drove up there twice a week, even in the winter. Her husband was all broke up. Me, too. When you don't have anyone of your own it hurts worse to see it.

Grid and Wally went maybe eight years ago, within a week of each other. I never saw them after I quit Mayo's. They both wound up housebound. I wondered if they ever missed the others they never even spoke to. Their funerals weren't much. Flowers, a few oldsters sitting around, mostly women with hands folded in their laps, soft organ music, how sweet the sound, nobody sang, nobody hummed. I wrote my name in their books and left.

Billy was the last, a grand wake downriver, high summer. A lot of people sat around the old Grange Hall on the hill and told stories. You could look off and see three little islets like arrowheads in the sun, no place to land, too small for any use, just solid rock jam-packed with spruce. I knew everybody pretty much. Billy'd been in the war, Iwo Jima, won two Bronze Stars. I never knew he was a hero.

Sometimes I feel like the empty tomb of Hiram Gooms. How could I not know one single thing about him, except his favorite place? I'm stubborn. I was determined to learn at least one other thing, no matter what, no matter how small, but I never did. No matter how hard I thought on him—and I still do—I've yet to come across one single fact, of any sort whatsoever.

One year I thought, what the hell, I'll make up a life for him, a happy one, too. I got paper and pencil and sat at my kitchen table from dawn till dark, and never could write one word more than Hiram Gooms liked to sit out at a certain, favorite spot of his on the railroad bridge by day and by night, paid his debts that weren't even debts, and got pushed off and drowned, August 17, 1967.

I had to give up trying to write him a happy life. I just couldn't do it. For some people things just don't work out.

This year, come that day, I picked a nice bouquet of wildflowers and took it out on the bridge. I couldn't do it at night. I don't trust my balance anymore, or my eyes either. I got sat down and yelled, "Hiram! Hiram Gooms."

He didn't answer, nary a whisper. After a while I yelled, "Here's to you, Hiram," and tossed my bouquet in.

Goddamned fool that I am, always was, always will be, the tide was running the wrong way. I got myself turned around, sat back down again, dangled my legs. There was a nice breeze and a little chop. My bouquet sort of bobbed along like a sly skiff that slipped its moorings.

I had to wonder then if I was the last person on earth who ever gave Hiram Gooms a thought. Maybe I was the only one for years and years, even when he was alive, and neither of us knew it. I wondered who his mother was. And his father. My gran'pa used to say, "Things near are far, and far are near."

In no time at all, my flowers were just winks of color in the sun, till I couldn't see them at all any more, nor even know where to look.

For a minute there I felt worse than ever. Then I thought, they'll probably just sink before they get anywhere, and anyhow Hiram can't see, can't hear, nor know, nor care, and as for me, I'll be seventy-five in September, and God damn it all to hell, I'm going to get the whole family home, I'll invite everybody I know, and give myself a happy birthday, like none I ever had before.

The Girl Who Saw God

◇◇◇◇◇◇◇◇◇◇◇◇◇◇◇◇◇◇◇◇◇◇

I t has long been accepted that a barbershop invites philosophical talk. Perhaps it is the rueful mirrors—or maybe the barbers themselves, wielding their shears, conspire to inspire it.

These days, here in Warton, one is likely to find only the old or an occasional child sitting in the town barbershop just off Main Street. The middling ranges go elsewhere or cut their hair at home.

Today, October 10, 1983, at nine a.m., two septuagenarians are having a trim, not that either much needs one.

But they have kept neat and clean all their lives, and it gives them a sense of well-being to perform the old rituals. And it gets them out of the house, out of the armchairs where they mostly sit, except when they help their wives with the groceries.

Walter Gresham especially is glad to be here. This is his first time out on his own since his heart attack. His clothes sag on him. He was a hefty man last time he was in, only three months ago. He always had a soft voice, but now the others strain to hear, and both barbers leave off snipping.

"Came right out of a blue sky," he says. "I nearly died. Ten days in the hospital. I never knew what pain was till then."

The others make their somber commiserations. Walter's barber, George Vinocour, is thirty-five, and probably will not look very different in thirty years, beyond a graying of his shaggy hair and an acute deepening of the lines of helpless empathy around his mouth. His forehead doubtless will remain as blank as a windswept desert, but he nods, he keeps nodding in a vehement way, never taking his glowing eyes off whoever is speaking.

The other barber, Z.A. French, is sixty-four, tall, slender, stooped. He has a flamboyant manner, a touch of formal flourish, being of an older generation. With poised comb and scissors, he resembles a sort of conductor amid the silences, snipping one out-stuck hair at a time—*snip-snip, snipsnip*—then tapping his tools together lightly and stepping back to appraise his handiwork.

In truth, for all that needs doing, the barbers could turn the pair of them out of their chairs in the wink of an eye almost. But there is no one waiting, and even if there were, there would still be no hurry.

The second patron, Ellery Wells, is frail looking, and had some difficulty getting into his chair and disposing his cane. He has a shy, kindly face and boyish blue eyes. A deep pallor prevails over the former ruddiness of his cheeks.

He does not come from Warton but from Birchfield, a neighboring town nine miles away. Since the Second World War, with the growth of the naval shipyard in one and the air base in the other, the highway between them has been built up, and on turnpike signs the whole area now appears as Birchfield-Warton.

He and Walter haven't seen each other in years, but in times past they occasionally met on the street. Ellery had been the Birchfield chief of police for thirty-odd years, while Walter had run a hardware store in Warton, which he had recently handed on to his son and new daughter-in-law.

Walter is amazed, remembering Ellery as a handsome, friendly fellow in uniform or sports jacket, who listened more than he talked, with hands on hips, always seeming to be leisurely looking off into the distance. Now it seems as if some force has drained him inward, sucked him down close to his skeleton and grayed his skin, though his blue eyes and mild manner remain eerily the same.

Ellery is sorry to see Walter's frailness, and reflects that neither of them is apt to live forever. They gossip a bit about the weather. It has been absolutely perfect. The famous stand of white birch between the two towns, somewhat reduced by inevitable encroachments, still shines in the clear air, and the lake shimmers. In fact neither they nor their barbers can recall a nicer autumn.

"After my accident I didn't get out for about a year," Ellery says by way of encouragement.

Walter cocks his head a little. His eyes narrow and his jaw sets, but he doesn't say anything, and Ellery in near disbelief says:

"You didn't know?"

"No," Walter says apologetically.

"I lost my leg," Ellery says, and taps his knee through the apron and trousers with his knuckles—an odd sound like a muffled musical instrument. "This is artificial. Nineteen seventy-nine that happened. You didn't hear? It was in all the papers—maybe not over here."

"Oh, yes," George says, and leans down into Walter's vision, nodding and nodding.

Walter is mystified. "I never heard," he said. He had been in Florida that winter, but he doesn't remember, and now he hardly looks at a paper, except to read the obituaries. The nightly TV brings news enough for him.

"I got shot," Ellery says, feeling the familiar shadow he always feels in retelling the story. "Down at Harp's Point. We got a call from some woman that somebody was bothering her, so Jim Wilson and I drove down. You know Jim, I guess."

"Sure," Walter says.

"We got down there, it's all woods, you know, and I stopped to look for the house. There were a couple of ratty little trailers and an old barn. All of a sudden I heard what sounded like a rifle.

"'I think somebody's shooting at us,' Jim says.

"'No,' I says, 'they're just hunting. Who'd be shooting at us?' I never expected anything like that, you know. We were just sitting there, looking around, and the next shot came right through the door, hit me in the thigh. I never felt anything at all, at least not then. I must've been in shock. I bled a puddle. That was the worst, that puddle getting larger and running under the seat.

"Jim finally got the guy holed up in the barn and called for help. He gave up pretty quick when the state boys showed up. Anyway, the upshot was, after about a month, they had to take my leg off. Early retirement, they call that. I was about ready, I have to admit."

"Jeez," Walter says, "I never knew."

"Oh, it was in the papers," Ellery says ruefully. "Thought there'd never be an end of it."

"Oh, yes," George says, "I remember," and he nods and nods.

"What happened to the guy?" Walter says.

"Oh," Ellery says, "he's in the pen."

"Too good for him," Walter says with definite volume.

"Things are different now," Ellery says. "I'm glad we lived when we did."

"Nooo," Walter says, "no fun anymore."

"I know," Ellery says. "I used to like the job, but these days, dealing with some of these characters. . . ." He shakes his head very slightly. He never moves unless has to; even his hands remain still.

"We never had any crime," Walter says.

"Oh, a drunk or two. Lost children," Ellery says.

"Where do these guys come from?" Walter says with scorn, bleak and indignant.

"I don't know," Ellery says. "Some of them are local, born and bred."

Snip-snip. Snip-snip. Every now and then the barbers punctuate a lull in the talk.

"My neighbor," says Z.A., "he lost his wife a couple of years ago. He never really got over that. Now he has to have a double bypass operation, so he can have prostate surgery and have his gallbladder out." *Snip-snip.*

"I help all I can, you know. He's a young man, only sixty-eight," Z.A. says, "but it's not easy."

All murmur and shake their heads.

"You know what they say," Ellery says. "Health is wasted on the young."

George says, "I never heard that."

Ellery smiles and says, "Maybe I meant it's youth that's wasted."

Z.A. too smiles. "If I knew then what I know now, I never would have lived this long."

The others' eyebrows arch a little and he coughs, embarrassed. "I'll tell you a joke I heard the other day," he says, and he taps his scissors and comb.

"There's three old geezers sitting on a bench.

"The first says, 'My sphincter's not working any more. I dribble all night, I go to the pot but I can't pee, and then I wake up in a puddle.'

"The second says, 'I wish I had your problem. I'm constipated. I sit there all day, but my bowels won't move to save my soul.'

"The third says, 'I wish I had your problems. I have a great dump and piss every morning, eight o'clock sharp, no problem.'

"'That's terrific,' the first two guys say. 'What's your complaint?'

"The guy says, 'I don't wake up till eight thirty.'"

They all laugh exaggeratedly, screwing up expressions of dismay and shaking their heads at Z.A., who grins.

"Better than not getting up at all," George says with jocular sincerity, and snips thrice.

"You should see my tomatoes," Z.A. interjects in a confidential tone, as if it might be a secret. "They're so big and red and juicy this year. I'm going to have one for lunch. I'll take one over for my neighbor." *Snip-snip.*

"Oh, yes, I thought I was going to die, too," Ellery resumes to Walter. "For a while there I don't think I cared."

"Yeah," Walter agrees with a gloomy grunt. "While I was in the emergency room they brought in a girl who'd drowned. She was legally dead, I guess—or however you want to say it—and they got her back to life again.

"I happened to be put in the same room with her next day. We got to talking, and finally I asked her what it was like to be dead." *Snip-snip, snip-snip,* goes George in the long pause.

"She said it was nice," says Walter.

"Nice?" says Ellery.

Reluctant Walter nods finally with furrowed brow.

"How so?" says Ellery.

"Well!" says Walter decisively, and then blinks. "She said she saw God." In the silence Z.A. goes *snip* after an eyebrow.

"She said it was nice to be dead," says Walter. "She said it made her feel good."

"Good?" Ellery says.

"Yes," Walter says. "She said it felt warm and safe. She said it felt like going through a soft tunnel, it felt good all over. She was surprised at how happy she was."

Snip-snip, snip-snip, go both barbers.

"Then, she said, at the end of the tunnel she saw God. She was completely happy, she said, but God said her time hadn't come yet, and she had to go back to life. She said she begged Him, but He said she had to live a while longer. She said she wanted to cry when she came to."

"What did He look like?" Ellery says.

"God?" Walter says. "I asked her that. She said God was light. She said there was a little dot of light at the end of the tunnel, and it got larger and larger until all there was was light."

"Light," George says, with a puzzled expression.

"In one way naturally I wanted to ask her more," Walter says. "In another way I didn't want to hear another word."

"I know," Ellery says. "You read these things, experiences people have and so on."

"Gives me the willies," Walter says.

"I don't blame you for wanting to ask," George says, and he shakes his head and the lines around his mouth seem to meet. "I don't blame you for not asking, either," he adds, and they all nod and laugh quietly with relief, discomfort, remorse.

"The way things are going you wonder if there's going to be such a thing as death," says Z.A. a bit obscurely, and lifts Ellery's apron off and makes it billow on the air. "Sir!"

"Beautiful!" Ellery says and smiles at them each in turn without glancing in the mirror.

He and Walter, also done, exchange heartfelt expressions of pleasure at having met and long wishes for good luck, take grateful leave of their barbers, and, having gotten down the two steps to the street together, go slowly arm-in-arm toward the parking lot—a frail, limping man with a cane and another, even frailer-looking, in clothes too large for him, who walks as if he is just learning how.

Z.A. stands in the window, hands clasped behind his back, until both cars are gone, and then glances at the clock. He sighs and takes off his white jacket. "I'll get us some coffee," he says.

George stands by his chair in the empty shop with nothing to do. Not even the floor needs sweeping. It takes half a dozen such oldsters to call for the broom, and they were the first patrons of the day.

At a loss, already weary, dazed by the thought of everything vanishing in light, he tries to recall his wife's warm hips and sleepy morning smile, wishes, wishes he too could hang up his white coat, forget his car, walk home the old way through childhood streets beneath the bygone elms, and take her back to bed for a long, long nap.

The Blue Stone

A Just-So Story

◇◇◇◇◇◇◇◇◇◇

For a while there, O, my Best Beloved, it seemed I was always doing one thing in order not to do another. I wanted to be a writer—I was a writer, if the act counted for anything—though what that meant beyond itself, I had yet to ask. After college I went to journalism school in Boston—mainly to escape the draft, but also to avoid academia. Graduate work in English looked like the direst danger life had to offer short of staying home in Bath, Maine, and becoming a recluse, so I set up in Boston, midway between Portland the familiar and New York the unknown.

Professors of journalism proved a raw contrast to the dignified interpreters of the great documents at Bowdoin. I soon fell under the sway of one Hal Hoolz, a swashbuckling cynic in a shiny blue suit, the only real newspaperman among his tweedy colleagues in communications research, a field just then coming into vogue. He had never finished high school and despised their degrees and abstract models, statistics, jargon, and graphs no less than literature itself, which he considered effete as well as unprofitable.

For a small stipend from the department I graded his daily piles of undergraduate news stories, wrote query letters to girlie magazines, kept his desk supplied with gin and Pall Malls, and confirmed his dates with the prettiest of his students, who wore a gold crucifix and never met my eyes.

Fanatics both, Hal Hoolz and I were bound to contend, though I was his only true protégé. The others in his advanced feature-writing course merely smirked at our furious disputes, while the clock clicked the whole class away. They looked on freelance work as a fool's pursuit: the real money was in advertising and public relations.

All Hal really respected was money made from writing. The enormous salary from this, his first regular job in twenty-five years, didn't impress him, and he intended to quit at the end of the term: work was simply too tame for him. He preferred to live by his wits, and could generate ideas as fast as Jasper Milvain. (He, O my Best Beloved, is an unscrupulous, triumphant hack in *New Grub Street*, a novel about marriage by George Gissing, 1891.)

Hoolz was ready to write on any subject whatsoever, no matter how little he knew about it, so long as he knew who his readers were. "First you analyze your audience, then you manipulate it," he would vehemently repeat. "That's all there is to it, that's all anyone's ever done."

"Even Blake?" I said, incensed. I happened to be reading Blake.

"Exactly," Hal said. "Blake who? And Shakespeare, too."

The row that ensued was the occasion of my first banishment from his class. He threw me out often thereafter because I always failed to follow his assignments.

His custom was to read the stories aloud and have the class comment on them. "This is completely hopeless," he would say two pages into mine—supposedly destined for *The Golden Years*, a retirees' magazine—about two filthy bums who decide to return to their families and freeze to death on the road in a spring blizzard.

The class would chortle. The two tall elegant Kenyans, tailored like English lords, who smoked Gauloises, had tribal scars on their cheeks, and never submitted a word, kept their benign expressions of insuperable composure, but Hal in dudgeon would hurl my manuscript over his shoulder and thumb me to the door, like a fed-up umpire ejecting a protester.

We never mentioned these frays outside of class, and I sat around the rest of the day in his office. To him the worst that could happen was for some pages of his to earn nothing, never mind whether they ever saw print: it hurt his pride.

He showed me his latest, an article on how to write a how-to book, maintaining that the ultimate subject of all copy is the predilections of its audience, concluding with a quote from Aristotle culled from Bartlett, edifying but at odds with his text.

I remarked on this.

"That's the point," he said. "It makes it palatable. Who can disagree with Aristotle? And besides, by then, they've forgotten everything I said."

He had a low opinion of the world of readers, but it didn't depress him. On the contrary, he was exhilarated. He felt like a lynx in the fold. "When I'm not writing I can't fuck," he confided.

He liked to lament that I lived in an ivory tower. At some inevitable point in our debates he always stopped me with, "Who are you to say what's true?" And while I searched for an answer he invariably clinched the subject with, "You should get a job on a newspaper."

He left in the spring, my attendance at the university lapsed, and one day I found myself adopting his advice. The *South End Gazette* had a dusty one-room office on top of a Chinese laundry. Its editor, Arlie Vindage, was just rushing out as I arrived. He wrote the whole paper himself, and yes, he would be glad of some help—if I could fill the bill. He gave me a handful of past issues and directed me to the nearest courthouse to get a story.

"Now you want to master my style," he said. "Pay strict attention to the way I write."

His glinting glasses flashed at me and then he hurried off.

That night, O, my Best Beloved, after a day at a district court, I sat down to his exorbitant task. He wrote a rambunctious, rococo baroque, obviously his own, though endlessly contrary to the tenets of his trade, often impossible to follow, purple, nay, gory as Caesar's last toga, obsessive, digressive, fraught with personal asides, gargantuan in its sarcasms. Bum puns ran ribald through its tangled syntax, and howlers and ad hominems abounded. Withal it had a lot of color and surprises, and folly rewarded was his constant theme.

He loved assault cases, especially those in which the victim battered his assailant, or a wife her husband. Calamitous lovers' quarrels were a favorite fare; also the shenanigans of alcohol and the downfall of thieves. He made everything funny, even the catastrophic. No one noteworthy appeared in his pages, only the normally anonymous who came to public grief. He was much given to psychological speculation on people's motives, their calculations of interest, their expectations.

So I chose the most likely case of the day—a Peeping Tom—and tried to imitate the Vindage style, assuming he meant to subsume my words under his byline.

It was a long, hard, discouraging night. I kept giving up, but at ten the next morning I finished a draft that seemed a fair likeness. Exhilarated and proud, I ran to present my three pages.

He sat down to read. I awaited his impressed approval, and my first official assignment. Gravely, kindly, pointing with his pen, he criticized the piece in a perfectly sensible manner, chiding the oddities I had written in, deploring my every deviation from plain prose. He shook his head. "Another year of school," he said, "and then come back. You're on the right track."

I walked home to my room on Hereford Street and sat on my stoop in the sun. The hours passed in their imperceptible majesty while I pondered what to do. My neighbors came in and went out, came in and went out. High overhead a cluster of stone gargoyles strained into space. As the days passed into weeks I found I hardly needed leave the block. Within two minutes' walk were a deli, a bar, a grocery, a laundromat, a drug-news-and-variety store, a doctor's office, and a funeral parlor.

I began to feel furtive. When I went home for a visit I didn't tell my parents I had quit school, and when anyone asked what I was doing I learned to answer, "Nothing," rather than risk further questions, such as "How many stories can you write a week?" or "How much do you make?" or "Where do you hope it will lead?"

I was continuously chagrined at how little most people cared about what I took for granted as prime: books, writers, and the writing of books.

The public notion of literature itself seemed to have died like religion and been resurrected in technical sects like westerns, science fiction, murder mysteries. To say one wrote short stories was to give the impression that when one grew up they would become novels. I set out to paper my room with rejections. The size of a wall, the smallness of a slip—even the most elegant, embossed and tinted—in time dulled the romance of failure, and one glum day, when I got six stories back in the same mail, I forswore the ceremonial bonfire I had planned for them, and dropped them in the trash. That night I caught a glimpse of myself in my window—a rich man's decadent son killing time.

Worse was the fear that while I should be getting experience of life, I was writing or reading.

My nearest friend, a medical student named Ned Stein, played devil's advocate cheerfully.

"Art is obsolete," he would say, locking his fingers behind his head, leaning back in his rocker. "What it does best is distress. We do love other people's pain. Once we get control of evolution and environment there won't be much call for it, I suppose."

He lived in a room almost as small as mine and did nothing but study.

He could sleep any number of minutes at will, and then wake up proportionately rested. He loved everything—skiing, fishing, sailing, books, his girlfriend—his mind aswarm with research projects he would begin once he had graduated. To him all problems would yield to the human genius, and he had a happy, eager look I envied.

For me words had become intractable enactments, and thus arose the risk of putting pen to paper, for things once written could never be changed in essence, but only revised in language. I would spend a whole day on a passage, and then, excited by nightfall's promise of women, I would type out a version that suddenly satisfied me. I would make haste to celebrate, and the next morning I would awake, head hammering, pick up my page, and realize that it was still unreadable, untrue, undone. Every phrase sounded like someone—Hemingway, Joyce, Graham Greene—and my auras, too, seemed theirs, in pidgin admixture.

I scanned the want ads, worrying about what to do that didn't entail desk-sitting, and got an ever-increasing stream of form rejections from ever more obscure little magazines with ever-stranger names like *Diceburg* or *Bulkeny*. The genus *Editor* I conceived as an éminence grise gravely weighing each page, till I got a condescending note with a returned manuscript and realized its author was no older or wiser than I.

My French landlady would come in and dust around me. Once, digging out my wastebasket, which was packed with balled paper like snow compressed to ice, she inquired, "Are you a deesparite man?" I squinted at her.

"I ahrsk if you are a disparette man," she said.

"Pardon?" I said, guessing she meant *disparate*.

"You are a disparate man, I think." She nodded firmly as if she knew the type well, and I understood with amazement that she was saying *desperate*.

I could read only slightly better than I could write. Afternoons I sat on my stoop and drudged through the famous intellectual tomes I hoped would explain life and the world. Everything seemed true and contradictory. I caught glimpses, but the next day I could hardly recite what I had learned. Nevertheless, mutilating them with marginalia, I read book after book with greedy haste and added them to my shelf like trophies.

One day, as I was struggling with Freud's *Psychopathology of Everyday Life*, a little black girl came skipping along the sidewalk and stopped. I ignored her. After a while she shot me with a water pistol.

I lowered the book to examine her.

"My name is Geraldine," she said.

I bowed slightly and went back to reading.

She shot me again.

"Enough," said I.

"Huh?" she said.

"I want to read."

"Why?"

I closed the book and inspected her. She was exquisitely pretty, though I couldn't judge her age. She wore a pale pink dress and her hair was parted and pulled back in pigtails tied with pink ribbons. Her dark eyes burrowed into mine disconcertingly. She giggled and covered her mouth.

"What's so funny?" I said.

"You," she said, and ran off.

I read another ten pages of Freud and then couldn't remember a word of it.

The next afternoon, about the same time, Geraldine came skipping along and handed me a bouquet of dandelions.

I was touched and embarrassed, but finally lodged them in my shirt pocket.

"I love flowers," she said definitely.

Thereafter she stopped every afternoon on her way home from school to pester me. I began to think of it as my recess. At two fifteen I would go down to sit in the sun and wait for Geraldine. We considered the world and agreed that fire trucks ought to be not red but orange, that ten-gallon hats could hardly hold five quarts, and especially that school should close early on nice days. And we played a game we invented called Watch Out!

I had to submit to a blindfold while Geraldine hid the blue stone. We had found it in the gutter, presumably dropped there—by a bird, we decided. It looked like something from a tropical beach. It was the size of a bead, with a deep luminous glow, as if it had a light inside. We puzzled over it. It seemed perfectly natural, yet was so flawless an ellipsoid, so smooth, pure and complete in itself, that it almost had to be human-made, but made for what purpose? It didn't seem to belong in a ring.

When it was hidden she freed my eyes and I hunted for it. Sometimes it was in a crevice on the steps, sometimes on a window ledge or in one of the crocuses that had thrust up in a corner of the ragged little patch of grass. If I went the wrong way she danced around me impatiently, insisting, "Cold! Colder! You're freezing!" But as I got closer she shrilled, "Warm! Warmer! Hot!" and when at last I was looking right at it, she would shout, "Watch Out!"

I would jump back in amazement and say, "If it had been a bear it would have bit me," and she would shriek with never-diminished glee.

One day I took her to the deli, whose proprietor I had dubbed the Robber Baron for his prices and girth. "Your girlfriend?" he inquired, always a wag.

"Yes," I said. "And we want two ice cream cones."

"Vanilla," said Geraldine.

"Large," said I.

Puffing and panting, he made up the cones and passed them over the counter.

Geraldine inspected dubiously the two lumps of ice cream. "Awful small for large," she said.

He blinked behind his glasses, sighed, took the cones back, and added an extra half scoop to both.

"Thank you, Mr. Baron," said Geraldine.

"You're welcome, little girl," he said, blinking back and forth between us. "But my name is not Baron: it is Papazoglu."

"You told me his name was Robber Baron," Geraldine said severely as we went out.

"I don't charge I don't live," he called after us.

We carried the cones back to my stoop. I couldn't stop chuckling with chagrin.

"He's a nice man," she said calmly. "There's my brother."

Across the street a neatly dressed black boy was going by with long strides. He gave no sign of seeing us, and she made no effort to catch his eye, but kept steadily licking her ice cream, twirling and twirling the cone to her tongue until he turned the corner.

"Put on the blindfold," she commanded. I handed her the kerchief, took her cone, with disquiet felt her fingers tying the knot behind my head.

"Little girls can be quite sexual," Ned Stein said, sitting on his cot in his white uniform. I sat in his chair. He was doing a two-week stint at an asylum for those who ate their excrement or thought they were prophets or never budged all day long.

"And then she's colored," he mused. "That complicates the picture. I believe the ambiguous dark lady is a stock figure of American literature.

"Of course it's natural for you to identify with minorities, since you see yourself as a superfluous pariah. Every act, every attitude, every human bond, no matter how ordinary, is symbolic. Of course one has to interpret. That's the trouble with literature: it can only assemble."

"What's the meaning of our hide-the-stone game?" I said.

"I don't know," he said. "Let's look at it."

"We leave it outside," I said. "Well hidden."

"Never mind. We don't need it," he said. "Obviously it contains a magic secret."

I put our conversation in my notebook.

The next day I made a rare trip home to visit my parents. My heart quailed at their solicitude. Mother plied me with my favorite dishes and complained that I looked thin. Father tried to pry out of me my plans. They believed education was the road to maturity and success. I didn't tell them that I had quit going to classes, and pleading exams I returned to Boston.

I brought a beautiful edition of Rudyard Kipling's *Just So Stories*, enchantingly illustrated by the author. It was a luxurious edition,

1912, with large print and a yellow frontispiece of a crocodile stretching an elephant's trunk. It had been the first book I had read through by myself. Mother taught it to me, her voice thrilling on the constant refrain, "Hear and attend and listen, O my Best Beloved," and I wanted Geraldine to learn "How the Alphabet Was Made," "How the Rhinoceros Got His Skin," and why "The Cat Walked by Himself."

"I just got *out* of school," she said.

I began to read:

> In the sea, once upon a time, O my Best Beloved, there was a whale, and he ate fishes. He ate the starfish and the garfish, and the crab and the dab, and the plaice and the dace, and the skate and his mate, and the mackereel and the pickereel, and the really truly twirly-whirly eel. . . .

I read on till I came to the small 'Stute Fish, the last fish left in the sea, which kept out of harm's way, just back of the whale's ear, and finally lured him in his hunger to a shipwrecked mariner on a raft, a man of infinite-resource-and-sagacity.

"What's that?" Geraldine interrupted.

"That means you can do anything, no matter how hard or strange," I said, "even if both you and your raft have been swallowed whole by a whale," and I showed her, at story's end, Kipling's picture of the great cetacean trying to take revenge on the small 'Stute Fish hiding under the Door-sills of the Equator.

Geraldine's eyes grew wide.

For the next month and more, O my Best Beloved, we made our way through a few of my favorite stories, and the hide-the-stone game was forgotten. Every line seemed to contain a lesson, and on the last day of school I gave her the book to read over the summer, thinking to try *Moby-Dick* on her in the fall. I was surprised by how loath I was to part with the book, and wanted to inscribe it with something commensurate, but all my phrases felt false, and finally I wrote, "For Geraldine with love," and signed and dated it.

She never came again. A week later I found in the downstairs hallway an unaddressed parcel wrapped in newspaper and tied with string. Inside was the book, its inscription blacked out with a felt-tip pen.

I was stunned by such hidebound cruelty. The book was old, fragile and faded, and I supposed some puritanical parent had found it offensive nonsense, or something not newly purchased, till idly leafing through the stories I had not yet read to Geraldine, I came to one called "How the Leopard Got His Spots," and my stomach fell into my shoes.

I knew exactly where those spots were at the end of the story—unthought of in years—that had bothered me even as a boy.

"I'll make 'em with the tips of my fingers," said the Ethiopian. "There's plenty of black left on my skin still. Stand over."

Then the Ethiopian put his five fingers close together and pressed them all over the Leopard. Sometimes the fingers slipped and the marks got a little blurred, but if you look closely at any leopard now you will see that there are always five spots—off five fat black finger-tips.

"Now you are a beauty," said the Ethiopian. "Think of that and purr."

"But if I'm all this," said the Leopard, "why didn't you go spotty too?"

"Oh, plain black's best for a nigger," said the Ethiopian.

So they went away and lived happily ever afterward, Best Beloved.

I walked the streets, gnawing my oblivion, hoping to see her somewhere. I carried the blue stone in my pocket, rolling it between my thumb and fingers as I walked my endless walks. In the dark of my room I ascertained that in fact it did not glow; only the sun's rays made it luminous.

Then to my awful disbelief I lost it through a hole in my pocket, and though I looked and looked I looked in vain, knowing all the while that if it lay out in plain sight it would not lie there long.

I resumed my afternoon reading. One day the locked door of the deli bore a death notice. Three days later the Robber Baron's brother, whom I had never seen, younger but familiar in girth and haggard face, served my morning coffee, alluding to a family malady that had killed their father and an uncle as well.

My landlady's other tenant, the girl at hall's end, who meeting me on the stairs always averted her face, began to have nightmares. Her faint cries woke me at all hours. I wondered if I could somehow help, kept deciding not to intrude. And the Boston Strangler kept killing, woman by woman by woman, while the sweltering city reeled from headline to headline.

I wondered what would become of me, besides a bum indifferent to everything but words. In dreams the future funneled down to an aperture the size of a period on a pristine white page the size of a sheet. I couldn't bring my eye close enough to see through to the other side. I thought perhaps there might be nothing there, nothing beyond.

Toils of the desk—spells of euphoria, invariable disillusions, incorrigible surprise that these reliefs were ephemeral, the ultimate inadequacy of every line—seemed at times a denial of all possibility, all meaning, all hope.

At the summer solstice I went to a party at a mortuary owned by the father of one of Ned Stein's classmates at medical school. These hardy souls studied night and day and caroused when they could.

We cavorted around the coffins in the showroom, to the tunes of a portable radio, and then descended with our antics and wine to a lower level, where the cadavers were embalmed.

Ozzie, our host, revealed these gruesome mysteries. Then the party reveled more than ever, and levity flew high.

Only I was apart and ill at ease. I felt the cheek of a corpse in a blue suit laid out in a voluptuous bronze-and-satin casket, destined for burial on the morrow.

Ozzie knew nothing about the man, not even his name, but the strange, formal dignity of his worn, swarthy, eye-shut face, the pathos of his red tie and gold ring, filled me with pity and gloom. My companions belonged to the world of answers, to stethoscope and scalpel, but already I was half-won to the secret zero behind all things, and reluctance beset me, a hunger for wholesome happiness. Then and there I decided to get a job.

I spent the summer, O Best Beloved, in a warehouse, a respite of sorts, while I read little, wrote less, but achieved the ambition of ending my virginity—not counting the women of Amsterdam and Paris—with the help of a black girl who passed me on to a friend with the admonition, "He ain't worth a cuss."

And the first story I ever wrote, in college no less, the most rejected, rewritten, despaired of, reappeared in the mail, transmuted into galley proofs from *The Lugano Review* in Switzerland, with a check for $75. I treated myself to a jubilant walk—obviously the pinnacle of my life—till I realized that it was only one, a number that somehow, by its flagrant fewness, now seemed more negligible than none.

In September Ned Stein returned to town with a celebratory pint of Scotch. He had been apprenticed to a laboratory on the West Coast, infecting mice with cancer. He had one more year of medical school, and then Life. He saw no reason why all disease might not be eradicated, in theory.

"Well," I allowed, "I finally sold a story."

"Hey! Great!" he yelled, jumped up and pumped my hand. I was amazed, I was always amazed at his happiness at all good things. I had never met anyone so at one with his life, so glad of others' good fortune, unremittingly eager to come to grips full-time with the enigmas of cancer.

By the time the pint was gone we were reeling with plans.

"And did you ever see Geraldine again?" he asked.

I told him the doleful truth, how I'd lost her and the blue stone both—both by inadvertence, both my own fault.

"I enjoyed having her around," I said with offhand dismissal. "I was hoping to get a story out of her." The idea in fact had only just that moment dawned on me.

"Oh, you will, you will," he said. "Never fear. You will. When the time comes."

He spoke so incidentally, as one who had long ago read my stars, that I caught a glimpse of my growing arrogation of despair that nothing I ever learned or did could last or have value unless it was written into reality, that blood dried to ink, that I should become my works and my printed works only—a dedication, Best Beloved, which led to so many of my future follies and regrets.

Ten O'Clock in the Morning

◇◇◇◇◇◇◇◇◇◇◇◇◇◇◇◇◇◇◇◇◇◇◇◇◇◇◇◇

There was no one in Hal's Tavern, so Ellis Willard and the girl named Emmy took the corner of the bar by the open door. It finally felt like spring, and when they lit cigarettes the smoke trailed toward the street, then suddenly seemed to fly off. She didn't inhale but squinted and blew puffs into the air, and then laughed for no reason.

"Firewater," Ellis said.

"No, please," said the girl, who was an Indian, "just beer."

"All right," Ellis agreed, "just beer."

"We drank so much last night," she said, "my head hurts."

They'd met the night before at the Hillbilly Ranch. At closing time he asked her home for a drink. When his whiskey was gone they went to bed.

"Hair of the dog," he said, clinking her glass.

"What does it mean?"

"The cure for one hangover gets you another."

"I know," she said, took a small, ladylike sip, and set the glass down. "It tastes good in the morning, doesn't it?"

He nodded, liking her. He had noticed a toothbrush in her handbag.

"Do you live around here?" It was the first personal thing he had asked.

She shook her head shyly, turning her eyes out the door.

"I'm only curious, you know. Were you born here?"

"Of course not." She laughed at the idea. "I was born in Quebec, on the reservation."

"How'd you wind up here?"

"I was picking blueberries in Maine. A whole bunch of us Indians always used to go, but when the season was over I snuck off and hitchhiked to Boston. So I've been here."

"When was that?"

"I don't know. A year or two ago."

"Blueberries!" he said, morose at his own nullity.

"It's fun. You don't have to work too hard. The man who owns the fields has two big cabins, one for the boys and one for the girls. You pick berries all day and have parties at night. It's near a lake. You can hear the loons."

"Loons!" said Ellis. As a boy he had wondered at their eerie laughter. Recalled now it sounded derisive.

"A priest from the town comes out and stays with the owner. He tries to keep the boys and girls apart."

"And does he?"

"No," she said, giggling a little, squinting out at the street. "Poor priest, he was all the time running every which way."

Ellis laughed with her. "So," he said, "what do you do now?"

"Do?" She wrinkled her nose at him.

"Do," he said. "Work."

"Oh," she said. "I go to secretarial school three nights a week. I'm learning to type and take shorthand."

"What for?" he said, stroking her black hair, which fell halfway to her waist, thick and heavy as a rug.

"I can't just be an Indian all my life," she said.

"Sez who?" Ellis said.

"My case worker."

"Ah." Things were coming into focus. "You should wear a ribbon in your hair. It would look nice with a red ribbon in it."

She wrinkled her nose at him, laughed without guile.

"When you finish your course," he teased, "you'll get a job in a big office building with little cubicles in it."

She looked at him skeptically. "I don't think I would like that."

"Won't matter. You'll have to buy things on time and make payments on them. It's called life on the layaway plan."

"I don't need any money," she said earnestly. "When I need something I go shoplifting. I'm a very good shoplifter."

A year out of college, Ellis still considered himself a conventional person, but living like a recluse without a clock in the South End, seedy and unkempt among derelicts and poor people of all sorts, had disconnected him. The rules he grew up with didn't apply here, and of his old opinions and beliefs few remained. "Just don't get caught," he said. "They'll lock you up."

She said, "They don't do anything. I tell them I just came down from the reservation and thought everything was free. Because I'm an Indian. They think I am an inn-o-cent." She spoke the phrase with care, each syllable distinct.

He had to laugh. "So you've been here how long? A year? Two? Three? I came in the spring of '59. How old are you?"

She squinted out the door at the green leaves, in silence—odd reticence. No matter, he had grown used to people's evasions, had learned how to find out what he wanted, in time, with patience. His hangover was gone, and he began to wonder where they could go to buy a red ribbon for her hair. The day seemed suddenly open to possibility. He had expected her to go back where he found her, never to be seen again. But here she still was. And it was spring after all. Wrong to forget that.

"Should we have another one?" he said in doubt. He didn't want to lose the day drinking, pleasant though that might be. And he didn't have much money. Soon he'd have to get another job, or at least work a few days or weeks, but he didn't want any more jobs, no more stupid jobs, one way or another, whatever he had to do. No more pointless work. And he couldn't go home either, not in the state he was in. Good folks, his parents, but worriers.

"Do you want to?"

"I don't know," he said. "Let's split one. Are you nearsighted?"

"I lost my glasses."

"Oh? How?"

She wrinkled her nose at him. "I broke them."

"How?"

"Willie sat on them."

"Willie?"

"My son."

"And where is he?"

"In the home. I go to see him every Saturday. They took him away from me."

"Ah," Ellis said. "Why?"

"I was living all around and drinking. I don't like to get drunk so much anymore. We could go see him. Tomorrow's Saturday."

"Well. . . ." Ellis said, startled, curious, a bit taken. "Maybe. Sure. Why not?"

She said, "When summer comes we could go blueberrying. We would be beside the lake, and I would show you things."

"That sounds nice," he said, stroking her hair. He tipped her chin toward him and stole half a kiss before she could turn—shy of kisses in public, he recalled from the night before. "How old is he?"

"Four."

Work, said Ellis to himself. No more work. But he felt pulled, pulled as never before—in truth he'd never been pulled in his life. He was just beginning to feel free again, though he didn't know this girl, and anyone can act nice. "Has Willie ever seen the reservation?"

"Oh, no. Not much. I went back and got him. I haven't been home for so long. There's a beautiful island I loved when I was little. We could stay there in August. In the pines. It smells good." She paused to get her cigarette going. He held the match till it burned his fingers, lit another, cupped it close. "Do you think that might happen?"

Her odd formality touched him. "Yes," he said—lie or not he didn't know, feared it was the alcohol talking, so little, a beer and a half, and dry, dry he was, knew she was, too. But at this moment he was happy and everything seemed obvious. Another disguise of a lie, he knew, and yet . . . and yet. What did he care for time? Work with a purpose perhaps. For the money, pure and simple. Wherever it led.

"I wish you could meet my grandmother. She was my best friend. She died just before I left, so I had to go. She was a witch—she had visions."

"A witch." Ellis started to laugh.

"She used to talk with our ancestors and make prophecies."

Ellis saw she was serious. "Like what? About you?"

"I don't know. She's dead now." Emmy pushed her hair back quickly, as if it vexed her.

"What kind of prophecies?"

"I don't know. It's all forgotten. They said I was supposed to inherit her powers, but I never felt it—it never did me any good, that's for sure. Indians down here don't believe in that anymore anyway."

"Do you believe in it?"

"Maybe. Sometimes I do."

"Let's split one more and then we'll go looking for a red ribbon, and something for dinner—my kitchen's a mess."

She made no response, smiling out the door.

A man in a shabby suit, looking as if he'd been out all night, came in and stood beside Emmy. The bartender came with a bottle of Schlitz and a shot of Schenley's. The man said, "Might as well give them a round, too," and before they could coordinate a No the bartender had popped the bottle tops, dropped two shot glasses under their noses, and was near to pouring the Schenley's before they both cried out, "No whiskey!"

"Pretty thing," the man said. "You old enough to drink?"

"Old enough," she said, with an edge new to Ellis.

"You Chinese? You mind if I call you a chink?"

"That's it, George," the bartender said.

"I was just asking," George said.

"I'm an Indian," Emmy said.

"You sure? You look more Chinese to me."

Emmy poured an inch of beer into her glass; Ellis didn't move a muscle.

"What kind of Indian?" George said, and knocked back the shot, gave an explosive sound of satisfaction.

"Micmac."

"What kind of name is that? I never heard of it."

She turned toward Ellis.

"Your girlfriend?" George said.

Emmy said, "Yes."

"Lucky you, pal."

Emmy was squinting downward; Ellis was scowling straight ahead.

"Hey, pal, how old is she?"

"Not your business," Ellis said—one thing he'd sworn, never get into a bar fight over a woman, never, it never could be worth it. Well, this jerk was big, but he was drunk. One good smash would do him, then out the door.

"Eighteen," Emmy told him.

"I'm twenty-three," Ellis told her.

"Pretty child," George sneered and stroked her hair She leaned away into Ellis's shoulder.

"You'll find out. . . ." George said in a different voice.

"What's the matter with him?" Emmy murmured.

"I don't want to touch you. You chinks're all alike, you always think people want to touch you."

Bald, fat-bellied Hal straightened up from the cooler he'd been stocking, came down the bar quickly, and leaned toward Ellis and Emmy, spoke earnestly. "I have to ask you to leave now. I'm sorry. Come back another day. Drinks on the house. I mean it."

They slipped off their stools and walked into the sun, back the way they'd come, not speaking, till he put an arm around her and pulled her against him.

"What's the matter with him?" she said.

"Troubles," Ellis said. "Who knows?"

"We don't have troubles."

"Only where we should be going first—red ribbon, I guess, then something for dinner tonight. Maybe down to Haymarket. It's a nice long walk."

"Okay," she said.

They slowed for a moment passing the Syrian Café, where men in broad felt hats seemed to sit all day, playing some strange card game. But then, as they were back again at Ellis's doorstep, by common impulse they wordlessly went up the three flights to his tiny attic apartment to take stock, get something, take a leak, make love, neither knew.

His place could use some cleaning up. He righted an upended chair from the day before, when he'd jumped up and run down to the street because he couldn't stand to read any more—better to be on foot, walking, walking, looking at everything. He came from Medford, nothing there at all.

Work, work, what work?

The sun blazed through his one pigeon-streaked window. She stood in the middle of the room, smiling at him.

"Let's take a bath together," he said, inspired and surprised.

"In the bathtub?" she said, squinting and wrinkling her nose as she did when she found him funny. "Do you want to?"

"Then we'll go for the ribbon and dinner. I'm not much of a cook."

"I can make rice," she said.

"The Chinese in you."

She laughed, came close, laid her hands on his chest, so intimate he drew breath and swallowed.

"And tomorrow—Willie," he heard himself say, "and then maybe on Monday we'll see about those glasses."

"I don't need glasses," she smiled. She shut her eyes and put up her face to be kissed, and he kissed her very carefully. The willing wet warmth of her mouth dizzied him and he closed his eyes and clung to her. Her arms tightened around him. He tangled his hands in her hair with wonder. It was only ten o'clock in the morning, the girl might be a witch, and somewhere in him he felt the foolish world shrink to size and a kind of colossal hope begin to stir.

The Other Party

◇◇◇◇◇◇◇◇◇◇◇◇

It was already way past his lunch hour. Stocky and dour, face crimped with worry, Amos Otis waited on a stool in a cubicle in the G.I.D. clinic of Boston City Hospital. A boyish doctor with latex gloves had handled him in silence, finally milking from his penis a whitish, yellowish ooze, which he smeared on a little rectangle of glass and then whisked away, leaving Amos in the dark as to what it was.

For three days he had withstood the sharpening pain, each night hoping it would be gone in the morning, but when the sticky discharge appeared he knew something was not right and went to the hospital, too mortified to tell his wife.

"Your slide was positive, Mr. Otis. It's gonorrhea, all right," said the doctor, returning from the lab.

Amos started to say they'd made a mistake, but the doctor just jotted something in his folder and nodded him into the next cubicle, where a white-haired nurse with a glacial face made him drop his pants again and bend over. "Relax," she said, swabbed both cheeks with alcohol, gave him a shot in each, swabbed the spots roughly, and then pointed him—carrying his folder in one hand, trying to zip his fly with the other—down the hall to a bench opposite a frosted-glass door with Miss Johns lettered on it in peeling paint. "Wait there," she said, and shut the door on him.

He walked guardedly down the empty hall, sat with care, looked both ways, and opened the folder. The indecipherable script intensified his chagrin at his prick's stir at the doctor's delicate touch.

Two shadows loomed behind the frosted glass. A Negro with a minute thread of mustache came out, glanced at Amos, and walked down the hall on his heels.

"Come in," said Miss Johns. Brusque and gray, in a starched white coat and pants, she motioned him to sit at the desk facing her, sat down in the swivel chair, and looked at him over her glasses. "Please," she said, and reached a hand toward him.

He transferred his folder to his left hand, bent forward, extended his callused right, fingernails grime-lined and cracked.

"Just the folder, please," she said, frowning away a smile, opened it for a split second, let it fall closed in front of her, and said, "So. Where'd you get it?"

He scowled—if she didn't know, how was he supposed to? "That doctor. . . ."

She smiled frankly, wryly. "I mean your infection."

Amos couldn't think. It was like being spot-checked by the cops, ominous with things unthought of or forgotten. He hadn't been anywhere in the last month—home and the FourSquare Tap, the grocery store, his sister-in-law's house in Methuen, his boss's truck, filthy little jobs all over Back Bay, joints rusted solid in cramped spaces, nowhere else he could remember.

"Well," she said, a bit tart. "When did you last have relations?"

Amos rolled his shoulders, not sure she meant what he thought she meant.

"Well. Who was she?"

He swallowed and glared at her. He could mop the floor with every one of them, no sweat—he was soaked as it was—he should just get up and walk out. "A man," she confided. "Men?"

Stupefied, he half-whispered, half-croaked, "What the hell you talking about?"

"A lady friend, then?" she tried.

"I don't have any friends like that," he said in bafflement.

"Well," Miss Johns said with stoic edge, "whoever she is, what's her name, and where does she live?"

Amos stared. "My wife?"

"Name?" Miss Johns popped the button of her ballpoint pen.

"Glory Ann," Amos said. "Otis," he added.

"Address?" said Miss Johns, writing. "Phone?"

"Same as mine. She's my wife. I already told you."

"So you did," said Miss Johns. "Have you had relations with anyone else recently? No? Then have your wife come in tomorrow so we can treat her."

"She must have a strain or something," Amos said. "She's been moving furniture around. She said it made her insides sore, all that lifting. I was at work or I would've helped her."

Miss Johns looked at him, delayed only a moment before saying, "Mr. Otis, you can't contract gonorrhea from moving furniture. There has to be another party, and when she comes in we'll have to try to track him down."

"I don't think she's been fooling around," Amos mouthed to himself, and then for the first time spoke directly to Miss Johns. "She wouldn't do anything like that."

Impassive, Miss Johns stood up, went toward the door, reached for the knob, held it, waited, but Amos still sat, staring straight in front of him. "Mr. Otis," she said. "Mr. Otis, have your wife come in tomorrow and we'll treat her. Now, you understand you mustn't have any contact with your wife—or anyone else for that matter—until you're both cured. You understand that, don't you? And no drinking."

Amos went on staring, his eyes fixed on her yellow pen on the blue blotter.

"All right?" Miss Johns said, and opened the door.

Amos got up, wincing at the drippage in his pants, and hunched past her, avoiding her eyes.

"All right?" she said, cheerful and kind, but he didn't answer.

A boy in a green garage uniform with a name Amos couldn't read stitched on the breast pocket jumped up from the bench. "Greetings and salutations, Miss Johns," he cried, doffing an imaginary cap with a flourish.

"Back again, Leroy?" she said. "Well. Come on in."

Amos reached the street, reeling with outrage, and punched the first telephone pole he came to, skinning his knuckles. By the time he got to the FourSquare Tap he felt ready to go berserk, his mouth a grim line.

"Howsa boy?" said Vinnie, leaning at the bar with Bob and the bartender, playing Roll the Pencil for a dollar a game. The bartender had just rolled another beauty, the pencil stopping label up not more than an inch from the line a foot away.

Bob said, "You get *all* our fucking money."

"You catch on!" shouted the bartender, and then quickly held up a palm of disavowal. "No, no, boys," he grinned. "You know why I always win? I practice at home," he shouted. He laughed his staccato laugh, slammed his hand down on the bar. "Ain't that right, Amos?"

"Whatever you say," Amos grated. He knocked back his shot, chased it with a cold chug-a-lug of Bud, instantly felt better, nodded at the bottle's speed-pourer poised above his glass. He knew everyone there, what they did, how much they made, who they were married to—he would be hassled no more today by doctors, should kick that whole snoop of nurses off his mind once and for all. He held his water as long as he could and then groaned over the urinal, one hand on the wall.

After that he stuck to whiskey, standing on the edge of the game, calmed by familiar banter, the crowding jostle and din of voices rising as the workday came to an end. His pain blurred and he began to feel himself again—why the hell shouldn't he, after all, with two shots of penicillin in him?—a man with a weekend thirst, though it was only Thursday. Well, what the hell!

But then he flinched to think. He just couldn't believe Glory Ann would fool around. She wasn't even a flirt, like some wives he knew. He pictured her coming to bed, wriggling out of her panties, leaving them on the floor. Afterward, on his way to piss, he'd pick them up and wear them on his head, breathing their richness, and she would laugh to see his ears sticking through. On hot summer nights, when she sat down on the couch bare-naked, she kept her knees demurely together, twisted a little at the waist, then placed her cleft bottom daintily just so, just where she wanted it to go, her back arched, eyelids lowered, as if she didn't want to let on that she liked how it felt, almost as if someone else were there watching her. He'd never thought of these things before, and now fear broke through his numb misery. She wouldn't, would she? She couldn't, she'd never. Why would she? He had the gonorrhea though—how could he have got it?

At seven Frankie and John the Greek came in, Bob and Vinnie joined them, and they moved to a booth, all talking at once about Bob Cousy's last-second, behind-the-back dribble and drive to the basket in the Celtics' win the night before, and him the smallest man on the court.

"I'm going to get good and plastered," Amos said, but no one heard. His instincts told him to keep quiet, but he felt hollow not telling them. "I got gonorrhea," he announced solemnly. "I been to the hospital."

All turned astonished eyes on him and he remembered uneasily that he was supposed to be contagious.

"I lost count of the times I had it in the navy," Bob said. "You aren't a man till you've had a good dose of the clap."

Everyone chortled. The word *clap* snapped something into focus for Amos, near relief, near pride.

"I don't think you're supposed to drink," said John the Greek, his eyes under gray brows smiling at each of them. Grizzled and mild, maimed at Anzio, shrunken to the size of a boy, he always bought everybody drinks till his check ran out, and then they bought his, though he hardly drank at all.

"No broad's gonna tell me what to do," Amos said.

"Amos Otis, you ol' . . . scalawag," Bob said. "I didn't know you had it in you."

"Lotta things you don't know," Amos said, rolling his shoulders in his shirt.

"Musta been a five-dollar hooker," Vinnie said with a big grin. "You're such a cheapskate."

"Like hell she was," Amos said. "She lives in a real palace. First time she came to the door in this negligee, she didn't have nothing on underneath. I played it casual, you know, I just went ahead and fixed her faucet, all it needed was a washer, these rich people can't do nothing for themselves...."

"Except make money," smiled John the Greek.

"So then she asked me if I wanted a drink. So I said to myself, What the hell, you never know about these rich broads. It was only eight o'clock, so I had all day. Boss wasn't too happy about it, but when I told him he just laughed."

Vinnie said, "You didn't offer to let him in on the deal? You coulda pimped her and made a bundle."

"So, where was her husband?" Frankie said.

"He's some big lawyer or something," Amos said, "he's never home."

"Amos, you old son of a gun," Frankie crowed. "What'll you do when he walks in?"

Amos cracked his knuckles, rolled his shoulders.

"Was she a looker?" Bob said. "I bet she was a looker. Amos, you lucky bastard you, with two women."

"Ha," said Vinnie, "what're you going to tell the old lady when she finds out you got the clap?"

"She's not gonna find out, right?" Bob said. "All you have to do is fight her off for a few nights till you're over it. Won't be easy, she's a tigress, I can tell."

"Unless you already gave it to her," Frankie said. "Stay tuned."

"Yeah," Bob said, "I didn't think of that. You better say your prayers."

Amos sat silent while Frankie told a case of his own, which came from his first wife's best friend. "Funny now, but at the time...." He coughed, drained his bottle.

Bob reminisced about the babe who'd kept him for a whole month in Hawaii. "Nice little shack. Right on the beach almost, nice little bar nearby, palm trees, coconuts, you could live on them, you had to watch out though you didn't get conked on the head, what tits she had!"

"You could be there now," said John the Greek. "Instead of this icebox."

"I don't know," Bob said. "I was randy, I guess. I wanted every woman that walked by. Anyway. I wasn't cut out for the tropics."

Vinnie described the awesome vaginal grip of this Syrian bitch he met right out of high school in Melrose. "She could make it ripple, man, both ways. I couldn't get my prick out if she wouldn't let me. She'd just hold on tight and laugh. When she laughed was best actually, and she thought everything was funny."

"A woman wise as well as gifted," smiled John the Greek, who claimed to have no tales of his own. The others teased him that they knew better, but gravely, respectfully. Their elder, he had joined up and gone single to the war, and single he had remained.

The others had enjoyed no end of early scores, slow-nodding at their memories of the bounty of youth. Inspired to surpass each other, to entertain and perfect the past. Their sex lives, so unlike anything Amos had ever experienced, at first disgruntled and finally repelled him.

"This broad's not like that," he said.

"She gave you the clap," Vinnie said.

"Maybe she's got a strain or something," Amos said.

"Maybe she got it off a toilet seat, too," Bob said. "Amos Otis, you been had."

"Like the rest of us," said John the Greek with tact.

"You had your fun," Frankie said. "Now you got to pay for it."

They snickered and smirked, a bit vindictive, rueful, bemused.

Remembering grinning Leroy in the green uniform, Amos sank in his corner of the booth and wondered what they really thought of him. Already they were back to yelling about the Celtics, his clap a laugh to them, his horny broad a whore. Resentment flared in chagrin. What did they know? He leaned on his elbows, head in hands, shut his eyes, and after a moment, she appeared in her door, in her see-through negligee. He wished she would just let it go, let it slide off her shoulders. Her shadowy Venus place made his penis ache. She turned away and went down a dark hall, glancing back at him, the gossamer nightie lofting out like a cape, concealing all but her bottom like two moons and her bare heels. He tried to hold her in sight, but one by one, feet, ass, hall, and cloth, all dissolved in a white mist, and were gone.

A vivid sense of loss remained. Who was she? Where had he seen her? Even a minute with her, he felt, would make good his trip to the clinic. He kept trying to call her back, but each glimpse was briefer, fainter, a memory of a memory.

The lights were up. His eyes hurt. He heard Vinnie say, "He's just trying to scope out his next move."

"Boy, do I not envy him!" Frankie said.

"She's a nice little wife," John the Greek said to him. "This isn't the end of the world." And however the others took it, they let it pass.

Amos and Glory Ann lived three blocks away in a hive-like, yellow-brick project. When they first moved in she'd had a hard time finding their wing, but now they both could have walked to the FourSquare blindfolded. The elevator was stuck again, and he kicked a hardened dog turd into a corner on the first landing.

Numb with dread, he trudged up two more flights, stopped to listen at his door—something he'd never done—heard nothing, slipped his key in, listened again, and then silently turned the lock, eased open the door, pulled it softly shut behind him so as not to wake Glory Ann, his mind fixed on tomorrow. He'd go to work before she woke, he'd make up some excuse for the boss, he'd work the day and not think, and then he'd come home, probably a little late, as usual on Fridays . . . but this Friday would be different, like no other Friday . . . and then . . . what then?

As he turned from the door he thought he'd barged into the wrong apartment—his whole day gone wrong—and glimpsed his broad in the dim light from the lamp on the table across the living room beside the couch, which should have been against the near wall but wasn't. The TV was in the opposite corner in front of the long crack in the plaster. The armchairs had been exchanged. There were new curtains over the kitchen sink. Everything had been switched around, even the immense armoire they'd found on the street and crammed with everything they had no other room for. The struts in the rickety chair looked to have been glued back in—something he'd promised to do, just never got around to.

Glory Ann came toward him like a stranger out of the dark hall in her bathrobe. He realized she'd waited up for him. "You smell like a brewery," she said. "Do you want something to eat?"

She looked uncertain, forlorn, not her usual perky self. She put her hands in her baggy pockets, feeling for a cigarette, her strained face brightening as she looked about. She said, "I hope. . . ."

He slammed her ear on the word with the heel of his hand, amazing himself. He'd never hit a woman before, and cried for shame.

She sprang up like a cat and reeled toward the couch. "Jesus, I'll put it back," she said.

He walked in blind circles, fists at his thighs, panting.

"Fuck you," she said. "I'm sorry."

He stumbled headlong down to the street and began to walk faster and faster against the cold, his chest seized with desolation solid as cement. He would never trust anyone again. But where could he go? He had no money left for a fleabag hotel, couldn't let anyone know why he needed a bed for the night.

He walked and walked, seeing nothing ahead. Unfamiliar cross streets bewildered him in his misery and rue; then they ran in strange relief into a dream of deep rugs and a perfumed bedroom. He felt himself exhilarated upward, past lighted windows of a tall apartment building, in a red plush elevator that imperceptibly slowed before a gilded entrance he remembered from a year or so ago, but the dim figure within, when the bars slid open, wore Glory

Ann's mask of grief from last week, that endless week of her sister's wake in Methuen.

Her husband had bawled like a baby, as if he meant to bawl himself to death. Amos was surprised at first, then embarrassed for Jack, who'd always made a lot of money and was always so cocky and sure of himself. As the days wore on his voice gave out and he just shuddered and shook. Amos had lost respect for him, though he'd wondered for half a second, What if it had been Glory Ann in that car, and him driving?

The thought came back now like a brick in the face. He stopped, put his hands on his hips to breathe. He was never out at this hour. The city was quiet, eerie how quiet, except for moments of faint clangor like the noise of boxcars coupling or the muffled thump of empty ten-wheelers bumping across train tracks. Shivering violently, looking left and right, he traversed vast intersections, the lights changing aimlessly into the distance.

He stopped again to listen, the only sound the catch in his throat. He couldn't remember ever being completely alone late at night in a strange nowhere place like this—trash-strewn empty lots, endless warehouses with no names, not even doors, no lightbulbs, no sign of purpose at all.

He turned in a circle—no one, anywhere. Shame bowed him, died away, came back as loss, like none he'd ever known. His groin's ache had spread through his whole body, and suddenly he needed only to lie down and sleep.

He thought, I've got to get home. I'll make it up to her. I won't tell her how I got so sick, I don't even know myself. She doesn't have to know either. I shouldn't have drunk so much, or I wouldn't've hit her. She can have things any way she wants, the baby, too, if she's really ready. I'll work weekends, and keep away from people. I'll keep a clean mind in a clean body from here on out. He jammed his fists into his pockets and walked slower and slower, half-panting, till he came to a full stop and stood still, stone deaf and blind, not quite able yet to turn back, held by the silence and his breath's brief billows on the icy air.

What Befell Her

◇◇◇◇◇◇◇◇◇◇◇◇◇

Drawn by its decrepit marquee, GIRLS GIRLS GIRLS, Rick Donovan first plumbed the dimness of the Risqué Night Club on Tremont Street in Boston early one Sunday afternoon in July, 1960, and wound up sitting with Dyanna Dale at the bar. Otherwise the place was virtually empty. From the way she kidded with the bartender, whose name was Charlie, Rick figured her for one of the regulars. He liked her easy manner—not at all grudging or shy. He kept waiting for the rebuff or hustle, which never came. She was just very good-natured and friendly, friendlier by the minute, it seemed. "Colored hussy"—he could hear his mother's cold indignation—"couldn't wait to get her hooks into you." Which made him mad, then sad, and, daunted by practicalities, he stayed only for the one beer, and then spent the next week dreaming of Dyanna's quick laughter and smiling eyes.

When he finally went back—it was a Friday midnight; he'd had a few beers—the place was full of mostly middle-aged men with pallid, upturned faces beneath floating veils of cigarette and cigar smoke, and there was Dyanna on the exact same stool, even more vibrant than he remembered, leaning back, calling, "Hello, stranger, I haven't seen you in forever," then laughing—apparently at herself.

Lifting his eyes from Dyanna's he was startled by the raw lewdness of the bump-and-grind striptease in progress. While he gaped, Dyanna said, "Don't go 'way," and slipped off her stool. When she appeared on stage in a glittering bra and G-string his disillusion gave way to the bigger shock of how stunning she was, and what a great dancer. He breathed slow relief when she left the stage without having bared any more of herself, or made a single suggestive gesture.

She was certainly the nicest, most beautiful, and youngest of all the girls, the rest of whom were white. The others preened and posed, caressing themselves, shedding their costumes piece by piece to riffs of the drum, and then for an illicit split second showed their nipples to a crescendo while the audience whistled and clapped, though some of the girls—they were women really—might do better, Rick decided, to show rather less than more.

Dyanna, who was only eighteen, had told the owner she was a dancer, period, which made all the difference to Rick. He respected her integrity, and her power to get her way, especially where money was concerned.

Ten minutes an hour she danced on the mirror-backed stage, as if she were alone on a distant star, and then she put on a skirt and top and sat with him. Between acts the girls had to mingle with the customers, and often the owner caught Dyanna's eye, and she would jump to join the clustered men.

At night's end they hugged and smooched her. She said she didn't mind, and Rick's outrage always turned to complacence as she got loose and came back to him soon as she could.

First thing the next day the girls cashed in their swizzle sticks—tiny plastic swords. The white ones paid a fifteen-cent commission, and the blue, for a double, thirty-five cents. Dyanna's bag always bulged with blue sticks, and she showed Rick how she let the un-swallowed liquor slide back into her chaser so she could consume a hundred drinks or a thousand. Businessmen tried to get her drunk, emptied their wallets, and stumbled away, she calling goodbyes, accent laid on gay and strong: "Y'all come back and see us again soon, hear?" Some men dropped fifty dollars at a time. The best spenders came in the afternoon. They bought champagne and brought presents—jewelry or gloves, teddy bears or glass figurines.

Some of them—gray-faced loungers with nonchalant money clips—seemed to have the fidgets till they got drunk like everybody else, though they still glanced when the door opened. Rick figured them for Mafia, which Dyanna confirmed with a shrug of distaste. He was surprised to learn that she was making five times what he was taking home from Broadway Shipping.

"I don't care about money," she said, "just so long as I always have enough on me to buy anything I see I want in some store window when I walk by."

Rick could sympathize with that. She was an orphan, had grown up in Alabama. Her father had killed her mother and disappeared when she was seven. She had always been more or less on her own. Her two-year-old daughter lived with an aunt in Baltimore, where she sent huge boxes of toys and clothes at Christmas. The father was long gone; she didn't know where.

By the second week, Rick had begun to spend every free minute at the Club, lunch included. He sped home from work at four, showered, gobbled supper, sauntered out again, slowly drove off, turned the corner, and burned rubber. When his mother asked, he said he was meeting Ed or Joe—made-up friends from work—one with an elaborate electric train set they tinkered with, the other with a great collection of 45s. He mixed up who had what, till finally he himself no longer knew, but she never seemed to notice.

"Are they drinkers?" was all she wanted to know.

"Just a beer sometimes," Rick said. "Can you loan me ten dollars till Friday?"

"He must have a girl," his father said.

Mention of girls made his mother glower. "It's a fine thing," she said, "when a decent young man doesn't get home until all hours every single night of the week, and then sleeps through Mass on Sunday."

"I go at 10:30," Rick lied. "What's the difference?" Judgment Day had grown remote, and anyway it was hard to see himself as much of a sinner. He would drive around, daydreaming, and be parked near the Club when it opened at one.

"You're only young once," his father said.

"Enough for anybody," she said, eyeing him.

"I have no doubt," he said, helping himself to seconds.

"Anybody," she repeated. "Bring me my bag." She found a ten-dollar bill, and then with unblinking scrutiny she nodded him off to his night's devices.

Dyanna was the most popular girl at the Club, and the others were always teasing her about Rick. They were tough-talking, but nice underneath, once you got to know them. When he came in they would say, "Hello, Baby Rick, how's Ricky Babe today?" and he would grin with increasing ease, having at first needlessly dreaded the annoying Rick the Prick, inevitable everywhere else.

At seven he would take their orders and go across to the White Tower for hamburgers and coffee. Some of the girls were just waking up. Until eight or so he had Dyanna to himself. They joked with the elderly black trio who never failed to tell him in a courtly way how fine he was looking, or they read the funnies or played dominoes with Charlie, who tended her end of the long bar near the side door.

Even after several drinks, daylight still glowed in the red curtains and a drowsy calm pervaded the Club—a time for gossip, for comparing Romeos and creeps of the night before, for doing fingernails. When regulars bought her a drink, they often bought him one too, and the evenings spiraled. One time Dyanna was gone so long to the ladies' that Rick began to worry. Finally she came back grinning woozily, and he realized how much they had drunk.

Mornings he would boast of his hangover to Shorty, his workmate, who would grimace and roll a bloodshot eye, his clean undershirt drenched by the time they'd been five minutes in the stuffy, labyrinthine warehouse. Shorty worked like a machine ten hours a day—two more than Rick, and Saturdays, too—and Rick had to follow him on the run from floor to floor, seldom waiting for the slow elevator, darting among the high-piled shelves, balancing armloads of boxes, then packing their maddeningly incompatible shapes into larger boxes, which had to be stuffed tight with debris and packing materials from jumbles of used cardboard. Shorty seemed to have more hands than a spider, filled more orders than any three other employees combined, and got the biggest paycheck.

He had a wife and four kids and went to the dog track every night trying to improve his income, but he lost steadily, made some back, lost again, and sometimes, crouched over his lunch pail, his mouth stuffed with sandwich, his jaw would stop, his eyes would glaze over, and then he would glare toward the open door of the office where the owners in short sleeves stood around a table, in the midst of which, among tossed papers and Styrofoam cups, a bottle of Seagram's Seven stuck up like a stump in snow. "I could use a belt of that," he'd say around the baloney and bread.

"Come to the Club some night," said Rick as he hit the time clock and racked his card by the door. "I'm always there, I'll show you around." But Shorty just showed his teeth.

Bothered by his own airy tone, Rick began to ponder the future. Warehouse work was okay for now, his first real job, but maybe he should get some business training as his father wished he'd done himself—and Dyanna should certainly finish high school, at least. Dancing was less than a job, more than mere entertainment, somewhere in between, but obviously, in the long run, not a good bet. When the *Globe* ran a series on the Voting Rights Act that Eisenhower had signed in May, Dyanna just scoffed, "How many of them's he signed now, three? It won't make no difference, no more than the others did."

She sounded so scornful it hurt, but in fact nobody he knew even seemed aware of the new law, which was all the worse. His parents revered Eisenhower the general, but not the circumspect president who presided over desegregation. Proud of the glances he and Dyanna attracted on the street, Rick had a constant, cloudy daydream of them uniting for a better world, but he could never tell her this for fear she would think him naive.

"You're much too cute for Dyanna," Kay told Rick one night, coming up behind and hugging him with a certain sincerity. "Someday I'm going to take you away from her."

He froze at the warmth of the woman's cheek against his, her reeking breath and diamond-tipped tits, and shook his head vigorously.

"You do and I'll cut your throat," Dyanna said, laughing merrily.

Rick forced a guffaw and Kay put her arms around them both with her head between.

"You're such sweet kids," she said.

Rick ignored the other girls when they were on stage, wanting Dyanna to know he only watched her.

She'd say, "Don't you think Suzi's cute?"

"Not really," he'd say.

"She's got a good figure for someone her age."

Rick shrugged.

"Men like a woman with a little weight on," she would say, patting her own sweetly molded belly.

"Not me," Rick would aver. He could have watched her dance all day and all night, too. She was like a goddess, beyond reach of applause, and the musicians, normally ironical and bored, nodded and grinned and played with gusto for her. The other girls as the night wore on merely gyrated in one spot. Their crude simulations of sex began to repel him, and thinking they must be nymphomaniacs, he was amazed to hear that several were lesbians and loathed men.

Thereafter Rick did sometimes detect a kind of mockery, a kind of assault, in their pelvic humpings, though no man he knew would ever take them for anything but come-ons. Dyanna's dancing was in no way lewd, but dreamlike and graceful, yet the sexiest of all. In truth she thought the life of a showgirl was perfectly ordinary. When she mentioned being nearly raped at knifepoint, Rick was so disturbed that she said, "I'm not going to tell you anything else."

He wondered what else there was, too circumspect to ask.

The MC, a raucous gnome who came on at nine, had a limitless supply of dirty limericks and lines, but he always introduced Dyanna in the same way: "Now here's a little girl that'll send you home to beat hell out of your wives."

In a single week she pushed a drunk who pawed her down the dressing room stairs; Lana's boyfriend, Timilty, a cop who hung around the Club and never went anywhere without his service revolver, broke her nose with it; and Sammy Solerno, quietest of the regulars, not seen lately, turned up trussed and garroted in the trunk of a stolen car in Providence, while for the next few days hardly anyone at all came around in the afternoon, including the owner—but it was the MC's unchanging words for Dyanna that finally made Rick wish she danced in a nicer place, and didn't have to mingle with pathetic lechers.

One pink-faced fool leaned so far out he fell off his stool. He sat on the floor, smiling and confused, until his concerned but helplessly merry companions heaved him up, dusted his suit perfunctorily, and pulled his hat down over his eyes backward. When Dyanna descended from the stage, they engulfed her, roaring like sea lions and slopping champagne.

In the men's room, where sour diarrhea fouled the deodorizer, Rick took a piss beside the pink-faced man.

"Does she go out?" he asked.

"Who?" Rick said.

"The colored girl you were talking to—does she go out?"

"You're crazy!" Rick shouted, after a hesitation.

The man gave him a dumbfounded look and zipped his fly on his way to the door.

When Dyanna sat back down with Rick, they got so hilarious together about the old guy landing on his ass that she grabbed the inside of his thigh for balance. He moved her hand quickly, in fear of deluge, but she didn't seem to mind. When she leaned into him, he always kept his hands off her, but fleeting hints of her female scent tinged her perfume and made tumult of his sleep at night. Lethargic at work, he would forget his errand, stop among the shelves, staring blind. In her bag he found a laundry slip with Mrs. Dyanna Donovan written and printed on it in different styles. He tried to envision what would happen if they somehow ran into his parents. He would have to move out if they weren't nice to her, wondered if they should set up house together somewhere, his mind lost in perplexity. He addressed to Denver a shipment meant for Miami, the mistake discovered only on the loading dock. "Best keep a sharp eye on yourself, my boy," Shorty said with dire lack of forbearance, and Rick realized that Shorty would have gotten the blame.

Rick's favorite day was Sunday. The girls didn't have to come in before three, and until the sun went down all motion was minimal and slow as in a rosy aquarium, the girls having a cocktail or two, smoking cigarettes and primping—they always had plenty to talk about. It was almost as if they were sisters and lived at the Club.

One such day, Dyanna arrived a bit late. Rick was halfway through his second beer by the time she tossed her bag on the bar and scooped out her handfuls of swizzle sticks. "Not a bad haul," he said, estimating the cascade. Charlie didn't bother to count, just gathered, dropped them in the trash, and jotted her total on her page in a ledger—it didn't in fact amount to all that much.

She seemed a little morose, waving off a cocktail. "Hey!" Charlie said. "You okay?"

She sighed, "I hear Cedric's back."

Charlie gave her a look and strolled away down the bar.

"Who's Cedric?" Rick said.

"He was in Atlantic City or someplace," she said. "I was hoping he'd never come back."

"What is he, an old boyfriend?" A painful question; Rick had no old girlfriends, not really. Dyanna was his first.

"Feels like he's my permanent boyfriend," she said with disgust. "No, no, baby, don't you worry. He don't care about sex, he takes me out dancing, he don't even get a hard-on. He just wants to show me off."

"Who's this guy?" Rick said. "What're you doing with him?"

"I don't even want to tell you about him. I'll take that cocktail now," she called down the bar, and laughed halfway like herself. "How I got mixed up with him—remember I told you I almost got raped?

Came right in through my window. Grove Hall, worst neighborhood in Roxbury, fights, crime, junkies, knifings, you name it. I didn't even like to put my head out my door, just run for the bus stop, get there, all these muggers hanging around, bums sleeping in the weeds, you don't even know if they dead. After a while I always took a taxi, both ways. Where all my money went those days.

"Cedric got me my apartment in town here. He knows the guy owns the building."

"But why go dancing with him?"

"He comes and gets me, takes me to after-hours places. He just shows up 'bout the time I want to go home. Takes me to Chinatown. I don't mind that so much. I'm always hungry. I have to listen to him though, all the nasty stuff he does."

"And you go? But why? Who is this guy? What stuff?"

"Don't nobody say no to Cedric. Specially me. He's an enforcer, he breaks people's arms when they don't pay up. He used to be a wrestler— in the ring—he weighs two hundred and fifty pounds. He keeps track every day. I have to hear that, too: what he ate, where he ate it. I have to hear his whole life. He lives with his mother, drives him crazy. He's so ugly you wouldn't even want to see him. I sure don't want him seeing *you*."

Rick might have been scared by now, but he was on his third beer. He said, "*This* is crazy."

Dyanna too was nipping away. "Crazy all right. Only man I ever met didn't want to fuck me. Only man I ever dated, anyway." She laughed suddenly, gaily, devil-may-care, straight into Rick's eyes. He could only gape, his mouth fallen open: she never used bad language.

She turned, bumping knees, reached for his far cheek—he had no idea what she wanted—and with her fingertips turned his mouth to hers and kissed him, full and wet.

"You're too nice for me," she said.

"No, I'm not," Rick said violently, and did as she had done, open-mouthed, clumsy, teeth-jarring, then held her against him hard as he could, his heart pounding.

"Ah," Charlie said with his best brogue, "Yer making me feel yung agen."

"Last thing he did," Dyanna told Charlie, "we down on Washington Street looking in store windows for something to buy me. Guy I know comes along, nice little guy, wouldn't hurt a flea. He's a mental patient, they let him out for the afternoon. He's so happy to see me, he say, 'Smile,' and takes a picture of me and Cedric. . . ."

"Uh-oh," said Charlie.

"Yeah," Dyanna said. "Cedric smashed the camera all to bits. Poor guy started to say something, Cedric pushed him so hard he cracked a display window."

"And what happened?" Rick said.

"Nothing," Dyanna said. "We just walked on."

"Probably didn't help your friend's mental state," Charlie said.

Rick was aghast. "Didn't anyone tell the police?"

"Nah, I doubt it," Dyanna said. "Nobody messes with Cedric."

"You should tell the police," Rick said. "I can do it for you. You're a . . . you're like a captive."

"You do that, you get me killed—you too if he find you," Dyanna said, and her downcast conviction silenced him for a moment.

"How about Timilty? Can he help?"

"You kidding? He and Timilty tight. You never mind, I can handle Cedric by myself."

"What do you mean?" Rick yelped.

Dyanna shrugged. "I just do what he tell me. I go buy some clothes, some cheap jewelry I give away the next week, he wouldn't know. I go to dinner with him, I ack like I agree with everything he say, like I think he a real big man. He drop me off at my apartment, he never touch me, never come up neither."

"I'm worried about you," Rick said, realizing he was starting to see what some people meant by real life.

"You the one got to worry," Dyanna said. "I got him under control. The onlyest time he ever got really got mad at me he said, 'I'd like to drive you out and leave you out on the highway with no pants and make you walk home,' but he never did it."

"You just be scarce around here at closing time," Charlie warned Rick. "He gets mad, you're gone. To the hospital anyway. He's got a hair-trigger temper, he's liable to let loose at any time. Speak of the devil." He dropped his voice, loitering toward the middle of the bar, picked up a glass, polished it, held it to the light.

Rick had an impression of a very big man in a knee-length leather coat: he had a square bald head, a seam of thin lips, and eyes like ball bearings.

"Hello, stranger," Dyanna cried gaily, "welcome back. This a friend of mine—Cedric, Rick."

"The Prick?" He had a low, granular voice. "Well, you're a nice-looking kid. Wouldn't you say?"

"He was just leaving," Dyanna said. "Nice to see you again, Rick."

"Nice to meet you," Rick said, getting up.

Cedric stared Rick off his stool and out the door. Rick sat in his car in the September sun, chilled by those eyes. He didn't want to go home with so much beer on his breath—Mom and Dad were usually asleep by the time he came in. It felt cowardly to abandon her to this thug.

For a minute he almost gagged; then he drove and kept driving, kept glancing at the clock, bought gas, drove out to Nantasket and looked at the swollen ocean, placid in the dying light. There were still plenty of people, plenty of girls, though not like summer. He thought idly of trying to pick one of them up, then despised the impulse. He fantasized about finding some way to kill Cedric, but how to do it, and get away with it, he couldn't think. He ate half a hamburger, threw the rest to some gulls, drank a milkshake, drove slowly around Cohasset, looking at the mansions and sharply edged lawns and gardens, parked again, dozed in exhaustion, woke at ten to a tapping on his window, rolled it down. A cop said, "All right, buddy?"

Drove home, drove all over Dorchester, while the clock stood still, finally went back to Boston, parked near the Club and waited, praying she hadn't been shanghaied. At half past one the girls finally straggled out, Dyanna walking fast. He let her go a little way alone in the almost quiet street, then drove up beside her. She looked around and got in.

"Where's Cedric?"

"He gone off with Timilty somewhere. They got business. He like Timilty better'n me, thank God."

Her apartment was hardly ten blocks from the Club. He parked and walked her to her door. "You want to come up?" she said.

Rick reeled. "You better not come up," was what she always said, and he'd been satisfied with the implicit promise. He'd never pressed her. It was always late, he'd had to get home. Shyness and uncertainty had made him docile, but now his need was fired with concern for her. They were in the same boat, too, now, unless he was willing to give her up. He thought, Am I in love with this girl?

She unlocked the outer door. They climbed four flights of filthy stairs with narrow little landings, doors at each end. The walls were stained, everything was dingy, but her one-room apartment was spotless and neat, as if no one lived there. There were some stuffed animals, and gewgaws and other trophies that must have come from patrons of the Club, but nearly nothing else. The huge mirror propped on her dressing table gave back the barrenness. He went to her window and looked down at the street— a pawnshop, a music store with a sliding grill, a cut-rate bar, a vacant storefront with a trash barrel in the display window.

She opened the refrigerator. "I got nothing in here to eat. Jus' orange juice, orange juice, orange juice. I'm not much for cooking. I don't have the time. I'll make you a down-home dinner sometime. Bad as it might be. I'll get my friend Tisha to do it. . . ."

He was puzzling the several wigs on skull-like stands. She pulled off her glossy curls. Rick was speechless.

"You didn't think this was real, did you?" She laughed husky hesitance. "I'll put it back. You want me to put it back?"

Suddenly she looked her age, looked, it occurred to him, the way he felt. "Oh, God, no," he said. "I like you however you are."

She laughed heartily then, eyes alight, mischievous. "Here, sit down a minute." She put the wig on him, adjusted it, groomed it, grinning winsome in the mirror, him breathless to hug and kiss her. "I be a redhead, if you want, I be a blonde, I be anybody you want."

"I want whoever you are."

"I'm me, baby."

"You sound so sad."

"Yeah, I am. Sometimes. But right now I'm starving. I didn't eat anything all day. Let's go get some ribs."

Rick groaned. She grinned. "I got a bear growling in my stomach so I can't hear nothing else. You be hungry too, time I get back. It's right around the corner."

She went out, no wig, tits a-jiggle in her short jersey that gave peeps of her pretty little belly button. He lay down grateful on her bed with his shoes hanging off. He worried the etiquette of it, finally took them off and lined them up under the bed, lay back full-length on the pillows, comfortably aching for her return.

What a day, what a day, not done, maybe not even begun. . . . He woke to a light tapping at the door, rose with eagerness like none he'd ever experienced, then stopped, and listened. The tapping came again. Again—then a peremptory knock. He got up, cast about, no place to hide, no fire escape. A key softly, smoothly turned the lock—and Cedric's bald head craned in, quick eyes left, then right. The door clicked shut behind him, his eyes for half a heartbeat fixed on Rick's. Silent, he stepped in and out of the bathroom, stuck his head in the closet, twice spread the hangers so crowded they sprang back like one elastic mass.

"So, little Mr. Prick, what do you think you're doing?"

Rick gaped at the ball-bearing eyes, measured the man's size in his knee-length black leather coat, agile and compact as a tarantula. Sheer fear, words inchoate caught in his throat. He saw Cedric's eyes note his sock feet, find his shoes under the bed, never saw the massive fist, bloody-faced on the floor gazed up at the ball-bearing eyes empty, incurious; then some shiver shook the man. Down came the eyes, nose to nose; hands grabbed Rick up, thrust him up high, and started him round like a slow propeller heading for the window.

Four floors down Rick saw the street, thought, I'm going to be killed, and cried terrified through blood and tears, "I never did anything to you!"

The going round paused; Rick felt his life hang, and then start round again, faster; then he was hurtled to the floor with a thud hardly felt; then there were Cedric's knuckles on the back of his head, curiously painless, then kicks in the ribs, thighs, neck, also barely felt—Cedric wore sneakers, for traction, he'd told Dyanna.

Rick almost laughed. Cedric, now panting, shaking his hands, stork-like rubbing his toes on his ankles, one foot, then the other, spoke down to him dismissive and princely: "I could have you killed for twenty-five dollars."

The door opened, then after a while closed. The room seemed full of breathing. "Cedric," Dyanna said, severe, sad, disgusted, "what you do this for?"

"What's that?" Cedric said.

"Ribs," Dyanna said. "I got us some ribs. You want some?"

"What's he doing here?"

"It's my house. What're you doing here?"

"He had to take a beating on account of you," Cedric said. "Rick, that's your name? You don't ever come here again, and you never go near the Club again. Okay?" He sounded friendly, as if it was them against her.

Rick half-nodded, trying to sit up.

Cedric took the bag of ribs. He said, "Put your hair back on," went out, and shut the door.

"Never seen me without my wig," she said, aggrieved.

She got Rick into the bathroom, sat him on the edge of the tub and cleaned him up.

"You a mess," she said. "My poor baby. You going to have black eyes."
Nothing broken, teeth intact, nose swollen, fat upper lip, knots on his head, now his ribs ached. He felt bruised all over, shaky, but triumphant.

She inspected him and began to grin. He said, "Wait'll my mother sees me."

"Don't blame it on me," she said. "I don't want her thinking. . . ."

"Don't worry," he said. It was hard to make his mouth work.

"That no-good took our ribs."

"We'll get some more."

"I'm not hungry anymore."

"Yeah, you are, you're starving. Come on, I'll go with you."

"You're crazy."

"I sure am." He was on the top of the world.

She put his shoes on and got him down the stairs like an invalid, and they made their way around the corner. Rick happened to glance across the street and there was Cedric, sitting in a car.

"Don't worry 'bout him," Dyanna said. "Nothing more he can do to you tonight. Be a while before he get mad again. He'll just spy on me and be jealous. Then he'll start buying me things again."

Rick felt more exhilarated by the moment, safe with Dyanna: they were safe together, at least tonight. He licked at a rib for show, while she ate them all. "I'm always hungry," she said. When they walked back to Dyanna's Cedric was gone, and Rick felt happier than he'd ever been in his life.

She went ahead of him up the stairs, very slowly, reaching back for his hand. Midway in sweet anguish he thought to catch in his teeth the jutting top of her jeans above the small of her dimpled back, halt her bottom's gyral commotion—but it got them there at last. She closed the door behind him while he stood in the middle of the room, knowing he should go home. She drew him to the bed as to a dance, dropped jersey, bra, jeans, and panties, then helped him open-mouthed, wide-eyed, out of his clothes, his blood-dried T-shirt abrasive across his face. He was sore all over, awkward, embarrassed. She helped him up on the bed.

"My sweet baby, don't be shy," she said, "only part of you not beat up, my sweet plum." And laved his glans slippery and quivering, then levered herself beneath him, and in it went as if it knew the way. In place of tears he cupped her face in his hands; she put her heels behind his knees, arms around his neck, waggled her tongue tip up at him, and they played slow tag out around his swollen lips. Down below he could feel her leaching all the heat of him, and then with a grunt she gave it back.

There was hell to be paid. Rick's mother had insisted on calling the police at about three a.m. and had been questioned by a calm voice, which asked, among other dire things, whether he had a girlfriend. "No," she said. "Well," the voice said, "if your son doesn't show up by noon, give us another call."

"Come to think of it, I think I did the same thing once myself," Rick's father ruminated.

"Not with me you didn't," she said.

"BOY," he said. "You played hard to get."

"That's how I got you," she said.

"And a good thing, too," he said.

Rick got home at seven o'clock, just as Mr. Donovan was leaving for work. He sat down and had a second cup of coffee. Rick confessed he'd been in a fight, though he'd got no worse than the other guy. Anyway, it was all a case of mistaken identity: the guy, who was very big, had hit Rick without warning, thinking he was someone else, and by the time it got straightened out they'd given each other a good pounding. They'd even ended up friends, or at least not enemies. But he'd tell them all about it when he got back from work. Then he groaned upstairs to change his clothes.

"He can't go to work like that," Rick's mother said.

"He can if he wants to," the father said, pleased at the son's spunk.

"You can be a little late," he said when Rick came down.

"I don't like being late," Rick said.

They went out and stood by Rick's car. "Now, tell me," Mr. Donovan said, "what happened? Your mother's quite upset. We don't want to make things any worse. Was there a girl? Or should I say, Is there?"

Rick knew that silence spoke, but silence told least. He didn't like denying Dyanna, either; he was bursting to tell someone about her, anyone but his parents.

Mr. Donovan said, "No woman's worth fighting over. It's always up to the woman. Let her choose, and be a good loser, if you have to."

When Rick got to work, it was all wonderment and jibes. To these he couldn't respond—he felt too tender about it. Dyanna's beauty he would have proclaimed worldwide, if he could. The others took his refusal to explain as sign of just deserts, so Rick the Prick revived with a vengeance. "All I can say is," wavered one between tribute and derision, "I hope it was worth it."

Shorty said nothing except "Take it easy, take it easy," and slowed down himself a little to show that he meant it, but then picked up his own pace to compensate.

The next day Rick called in sick. He now felt the way he looked, his face like brittle cement, his elation gone. He dozed between ice packs and hot washcloths, terrors of Cedric, need for Dyanna's nakedness, thoughts of eloping with her, of never coming back. When his mother went out he limped downstairs to the phone, but Dyanna didn't answer. She never answered her phone; the phone, she'd said, was only trouble—Cedric, or the Club wanting her to fill in for someone, or to come pronto and entertain favored patrons. "Popular demand," said the unsmiling owner, who acted as if Rick didn't exist. Dyanna didn't know Rick's number, would never have called Rick at home anyhow. The girls could take calls at the Club until five, but this was her day off, laundry day. She had an astonishing wardrobe, and a huge dry-cleaning bill, never wore the same outfit twice. He lay back down, trying to think of what he knew about her—almost nothing, in fact. Her daughter's name? Perhaps she'd told him, and he'd forgotten. Her child was as unreal to him as his made-up friends, Joe and Ed.

Mr. Donovan came home early and took Rick to his favorite place, the Green Deal Tavern. Rick ordered a ham sandwich and a Guinness on draft, which he quaffed before their food came; he then asked, and received permission, to have another. "Best in the world," said Mr. Donovan, who hadn't had a drink since Rick was born. "Tell me about your girl."

And Rick told—that she was colored—and skipped the rest. "I'm sure she's very nice," Mr. Donovan said. "She must be, if you like her. And she likes you."

Rick was surprised by the casual tone of his never-intrusive father, who pursued: "And do you . . . are you intimate?"

"Once," Rick said, and recalled with wonder Two, Three and Four. He could feel her all over him.

"She's not pregnant, is she?" Mr. Donovan said, sensing that there must be more.

"No," Rick said. "Definitely not." Then wondered.

"Because you must take care," Mr. Donovan said. "Your mother and I, we didn't until our wedding night. Things are different now, I know. Wild oats, they used to call it. I don't know. You take life as it comes, I guess, while you can. But you're a man now, you're practically on your own. If you've embarked on something serious with her—I hope you haven't, I hope you won't—but if you have, if you do, you've got to be fair to her. Wild oats is for the rich. And be prepared. . . ."

Rick had never seen his father so sympathetic or so grave; certainly he'd never heard mention of a wedding night—he shied from the thought—whence, it occurred to him, he might himself have come.

"In the heat of the moment," Mr. Donovan said, "you can forfeit all choice. Forever. You must think carefully—for both of you. We won't speak of this. Your mother loves you. She worries. She has her point."

Rick went back to bed and brooded. Over the next few days the future shrank before the onslaught of the immediate. Rick managed two brief phone contacts—when he started to say how much he missed her, she said, "I can't talk now, I gotta go." In the second, she just sounded resigned: "Yeah, Cedric in and out all the time, he more or less live here, walks me home at night. At least don't nobody else bother me."

Rick said, "Ask him for the name of his hit man, I'll go fifty," but she didn't laugh.

In the mirror he still looked, as his mother said, "like the wrath of God." The week at work was exhausting, Shorty tireless, annoyed by Rick's apologies for being so clumsy and slow. More and more anxious, on Wednesday's lunch hour he caught Dyanna at the crowded laundromat, wigless, preoccupied, neatly folding each item with a critical eye. He was the only man there, aware of impassive glances, awkward as a bill collector.

Asked about Cedric she shrugged as if he were like the weather, to be put up with.

"I'd like to take you away somewhere," Rick said, trying to regain some accord.

"Where you going to take me?" she said. "You ain't going to take me anywhere."

"I wish I could."

She stopped to look at him, her face softening, said, "I wish you could," resumed folding, sad-faced. In her shapeless housedress, engrossed in packing her basket, she looked, Rick thought, like someone he might never have noticed on the street. He wanted to touch her back to him somehow, but in the sun-dimmed fluorescence amid all the eyes there seemed no way. He was unused to her except at the Club beside him enclosed in the dark, drinking toward intimacy—and that one night in her bed. She hadn't even mentioned his still-lumpy, empurpled face. He said, "You should get your lock changed."

"I tole you, the owner's tight with Cedric. He'd want to know why I want a new lock. He'd give Cedric a key anyway. Lock's no good anyway, he'd just break down the door. Anyway he won't ever come in there again unless he think you're in there."

Rick said, "I wish there was some way we could get rid of him."

"Me, too," she said. "Go find someone mean as Cedric."

He said, "I'd give you a ride, but I've got to get back to work."

"That's all right, baby," she said. "My favorite taxi man be along in a while, when he have the chance. He drive me everywhere, no charge."

"I'll see you at the Club then," Rick said. "Soon."

"Okay, baby," she said into the dryer, then turned and said louder, "Bye, Rick."

"Bye, Dyanna," he called through the closing door.

Over the next three days the eyes of Cedric, his father, and Shorty pinned Rick into such a swivet that he began to think maybe he should just join the army, rather than wait on the draft: that way at least he could pick a specialty. On Sunday morning, though, he woke cool and decided. At one o'clock he parked in sight of the Club, hoping to intercept Dyanna and make a plan about how and where they could meet. By three o'clock several of the girls had come in, and ten or a dozen men. He went in and stood at the bar.

Charlie said, "She hasn't come in yet."

He forced himself to sit down, but she kept not coming in, and it was dismal waiting inside, not drinking, just sitting there, so he went out and sat in the car. What he would do if Cedric appeared he didn't know; he thought it would probably be all right if Dyanna wasn't there. If Cedric walked in on them both—well, that must be avoided. So he sat in his car, then got so restless that he had to step inside again. The fourth time he opened the door halfway, Charlie gave half a shake of the head, and he never had to cross the threshold.

By eight o'clock he was exhausted from tension, ready to give up, gazing the other way, when he saw Dyanna enter the Club in a sweater and skirt with a light wrap of an older style than he had ever seen on her, womanly almost, more beautiful, strange and mysterious.

He counted out an exacting minute, one-and, two-and, three-and....
Then he went in, sat down beside her, and said, amazed at his suavity,
"May I buy you a drink, Miss? May I take you away?"

She looked a bit stricken. "I took the night off," she said. "Maybe
you better not wait."

She was wearing earrings and a necklace of green stones. He was
fixated on these, his mind a whirl of foreboding about her favorite
taxi driver, when a man sat down beside him, blessedly not Cedric, a
black man exceedingly well dressed, a little gray at the temples, and
handsome and pleasant as a movie star.

"Rick," Dyanna said, "this is Thomas."

"Jordan," the man said, offering his manicured hand, which Rick
shook.

Thomas Jordan made fluent chat with Rick about how nice Dyanna
looked, as if she and Rick were brother and sister, getting irresistible
grins from them both, Rick's stomach sinking into his shoes withal.

Finally, gravely, Thomas Jordan consulted his watch, a very expen-
sive watch, and said, "I suppose, my dear, that we should go. I'm glad
to have met you," he said to Rick, and stood up.

"Thanks," Rick said. "Me, too." And stood up.

Bowed, eyes down, nunlike, Dyanna went in silence. Thomas Jordan followed, saying to Charlie, "Give him whatever he'd like."

It shocked Rick to realize that Thomas Jordan was the only Negro
he'd ever seen in the Club, except for the band, and a woman or two,
now he thought of it. His sense of loss was so complete that for the
next week he never left the house after supper and could hardly get
himself out of bed for work. One morning in the mirror he noted
that most signs of Cedric were gone from his face, though his eyes
seemed somehow different. The night after Thanksgiving he went
back to the Club, hoping perhaps that Thomas Jordan had been a
passing thing, surprised to feel no dread of Cedric.

"Hello, stranger," Suzi said. "How nice to see you." Coming down
from the stage, she stopped to talk with him, gauzy lingerie, fringes

and frills, in one arm. She said Dyanna didn't come around anymore, just once in a while to say hello. She was dancing at the Big C, out in Roxbury.

"What's the C stand for?" Rick wondered.

"I don't know. It's Thomas Jordan's plaything. He's in some big racket or other. I used to go out there when I was sweet on somebody."

"I should go see her," Rick said.

"Oh, you can't go there."

"And you can?"

"I'm a woman."

"What about Cedric?"

"Him either. No one's going to bother her out there."

"What's he going to do?"

"Eat his heart out," Suzi said. "He never comes around anymore. Dyanna always asks after you. She liked you a lot."

Rick sighed with gratitude, then sagged involuntarily.

"We all miss you," Suzi said. "I do, too."

Rick knew she had always liked him—she'd never let it show, but warmth had always palpably flowed from her, and now it went straight to his heart. He liked her compact fullness. He'd always kept away from her because of that attraction, which now bloomed in freedom.

"Anyway," Suzi said, "she's making a lot more money, and she can dance when she wants to, or not."

"Does she have to socialize?"

"She'll never have do that again." Suzi stepped closer, nearly naked, nearly in his arms. "I'll give you a little, take your mind off Dyanna for a while, maybe all the way off, maybe. I'd like to try."

It was so wistful, so humbly said, that Rick realized he could slide his hand down her backside and inside her G-string and she would offer her wetness, just standing there, right there at the bar. He was shocked by how dear she was, how overwhelmingly kind and true, and once home he wished he'd let it happen, wanted, wanted, wanted to go back, but he didn't.

After work the next day he stood across the street from Dyanna's narrow apartment building and looked up at the window that he'd expected to be thrown through. Nothing could be seen. With painful, vague purpose he crossed, rang, got buzzed in, and found the name A. Alden on her mailbox.

He never went back to the Club. And he never tried to see Suzi again. It just didn't feel right.

Thoughts of Dyanna gave him such pain that he never again spoke her name aloud, even to himself, and his father never asked. A year later he met an Irish girl whose charming freckles came out like stars in the morning, faded throughout the day, and disappeared at night. She occasionally jarred him by her resemblance to his mother; she married him and made him twice a father.

Ten years later, after his divorce, he drove through the district once at high noon and found bulldozed rubble where the nightclub had been. He parked and got out. Dust swirled and windblown newspapers clung to the chain-link fence.

First love was nothing, he thought bitterly, but a buried secret—as if it never had been.

His second wife got him off the booze and back to church. He remembered the day he first walked into the Club with no one there but Dyanna and Charlie. They had seemed to be the only people he needed in the whole world, the Club the only place he wanted to be. He could see her clearly now, could see himself, had out-wept sorrow, lived down remorse. What befell her was the one mystery his life would never solve: of everything else he knew as much as he cared to know, and all too often more. At Mass that Sunday he prayed for her. And he prayed for her daughter.

In the Dunes

◇◇◇◇◇◇◇◇◇◇

The motel party had run out of everything but green Chartreuse.

"This is not my scene," Sabrina said. "Not my scene at all."

"Back to town?" said Jeff.

"I couldn't," Sabrina said. "I'm too tired to do anything but keep going."

Eddie was sitting on the floor with a woman in a gold miniskirt who was explaining the mechanics of quicksand—the more you struggle, the more you sink. Her husband had nearly been swallowed whole. He'd gone down all the way up to his chin before someone came along with a rope.

"Which was worse yet," she said. "Like getting garroted in slow motion."

"Whoa there!" said Eddie.

"I swear," she said. "On a stack of *Bibles*."

Eddie snorted.

Diehards clustered in doorways, glanced up at the starless sky, went back in, came back out.

"All these scruffy people with their sunburns," Sabrina said.

"So, what are we waiting for?" Jeff said. He and Eddie had just graduated from Oberlin. Hearing that Provincetown in summer was one perpetual party, they'd closed their bottomed-out bank accounts, tossed some camping gear into Eddie's rust-bucket van, driven nonstop, arrived in time to drink coffee on the beach at sunrise, and by noon had found a cheap rental in a converted chicken coop with two cots and a hot plate.

Next day Eddie got a dishwashing job at Howard Johnson's and Jeff set up his typewriter under their one window, whereupon the town's vaunted hedonism made instant disciples of them, with the sole difference that once Eddie was done with work he was done, whereas Jeff was always un-begun.

Sabrina faked a smile. "You're both so boring. I hate men who bore me." She dropped her skirt and dove into the pool. Jeff stripped to his shorts and dove in after her. For a moment she let him suck her nipples through her thin top.

He was just getting a hand down her panties when the manager appeared. "Please," he said. "It's after midnight. I've been nice, but if you're not guests here you've got to go now."

Jeff collected Eddie, and they stood smoking by his van, waiting for Sabrina to swipe a towel.

"Interesting specimen," Eddie said.

"If I'm going to write tomorrow. . . ." Jeff said.

"It's still tonight," Eddie said.

Jeff had written some stories and poems in college but had never finished anything substantial on his own. Summers he had made starts on three different novels, none of which could he now stand to face in memory, nor could he recall exactly how any of them had been intended to end, except in broad, ironical deserts yet to be dreamed up.

Sometimes just to compose a plausible scene felt beyond him: always things were wrong with it, things unreal, askew, improbable. Personal humiliations had begun to accumulate. This night he noticed his glasses had become so dirty it was like peering through a fog. He'd let them slide down his nose so he could look over them. Keeping his head slightly bent with his eyebrows raised made him feel authorial, but when he went to piss they fell into the toilet.

Eddie didn't know what he wanted to do, didn't really want to do anything, thought he might just stay on the road for a year or two, keep clear of his draft board, be a beatnik, why not? All you really needed was food, warm weather, and a girl with money.

Sabrina emerged from one of the doors, tousling her hair. "Souvenir," she called, and tossed her wrung-out panties at a staring boy who looked thirteen. "Let's go to Sasha's," she said. "Their parties go till dawn."

Eddie and Jeff waited for each other to speak. Finally Jeff said, "You don't have to be at work till six." H.J.'s was where they ate all their meals, when they weren't in their chicken coop boiling rice or frying eggs.

"Plenty of time," Eddie said. "Plus I don't have to go in. I can just be sick and tired."

The three squeezed into the van. "I want to see Sasha—he's gorgeous," Sabrina said. "You'll love these people. They're the most beautiful people in the world. Sasha had a successful book a few years ago . . . well, ten or so, maybe fifteen. It almost won a prize, I forget what. There was a row among the jurors. Next thing to a controversy. Wait till you see his wife, she's absolutely gorgeous, she's his sixth, she has a seventeen-year-old daughter who's gorgeous, too. And very promiscuous, I understand. You should bed her, Jeffrey."

"Sounds right up our respective alleys," Eddie said.

Sabrina bit Jeff on the shoulder.

"Ow," he said. "What's that for?"

"I bite people," she said, "because I like to bite people like you."

"All right," he said. "Okay by me." He tried to wrestle an arm around her, and she bit him again.

"I wonder if you'd care to be raped," he said.

"Don't be crass," she said. "Besides, I didn't wear my diaphragm."

"Time of the month?" Eddie said.

"Left," Serena said. "Go left, young man."

They turned onto the highway and drove in the rattling van through the murky, stifling night.

"How far is this place?" Eddie kept saying. "Where is this place?"

Sabrina kept saying, "You'll see. We're almost there."

"Jeff's taking a little snooze," Eddie said.

"Keep him out of trouble," Sabrina said.

Jeff heard each word, unmoored in the night. After a while he felt the van veer onto a winding sand road and then after a spell of jouncing make yet a third left with such a lurch that his eyes flew open on a narrow track that meandered through brushing bushes like a tunnel; suddenly they emerged in the dunes, nothing visible, desolate black dark around the feeble headlights. "Where the hell are we?" he said.

"Here," Sabrina said. "Where do you think? You're so stupid. Wake up," she said, and bit him, this time hard enough to hurt. He tried to constrain her but she was like a tangle of eels.

In the distance, coming closer, was a high knob topped with what looked like a church. The circuitous way led up and up, became broken asphalt and then crushed rock, went up more steeply, engine roaring, and then wound around and ended on a flat summit beside a ramshackle, high-gabled facsimile of a minuscule Victorian mansion, obviously humoresque, uniquely out of place, with a dozen cars or so parked around it and a long, low sports car cloaked in a form-fitting sheath, like a prize torpedo.

"It's practically an antique," Sabrina said. "It's worth a fortune. Sasha loves that car, he used to race all over Europe. He's been promising me a ride in it ever since I was a kid. He never, ever takes anyone with him, not even his wives, or so he claims."

"Money there all right," Eddie said.

"Oh, Sasha's rich," Sabrina cried. "Rich! Rich!"

From where they stood nothing could be seen in any direction.

"Must be quite a view when the sun's out," Jeff said.

"If you'd shut up you could hear the surf," Sabrina said. She strode toward the far side, where a circuitous path led around and down. A toy house stood in a faint glow of light at the bottom of the pit. Voices drifted up from the open windows.

Eddie and Jeff followed her down. The walls rose around them like a dead volcano. There was not a breath of air; it was hot, then hotter. By the time they reached the bottom Sabrina had gone in.

"Sabrina, Sabrina Talebe," a woman's vice dwelt. "How dreadfully nice! What brings you here?"

"I heard you were having a party," she said, sounding young.

"How dreadfully nice of you to come," said the voice.

Eddie and Jeff fortified themselves at the doorside table of spirits—no beer, only remnants of ice melt and various bottles. Neither was eager to wade into a crowd of proprietary elders.

At a distance, out of the light, two men reclined in the sand, their cigarettes burning red, then dying away. "Like a purgatory party," Jeff quipped when Sabrina came back out.

"You're out of your league," she said. "That's everybody you ever wanted to be."

"Which is who?" Eddie scoffed.

"Not you—you go in, just say you got lost," she said, and gave him a push. "Come," she said to Jeff and led him to the two men, one of whom appeared to be a giant.

"This is Sasha," she said.

"Welcome." He wore only a pair of large, loose khaki shorts, had the deep tan of one who lives in the sun. "Tony Dimes," he nodded at the other. "Sit, for Chrissakes."

Jeff sat, fished for a cigarette, found none. Tony Dimes offered his pack, then a light.

"He wants to be a writer," Sabrina said with amused hauteur, "*and* go to bed with me."

"Whatever for?" Sasha said.

She looked a bit hapless, a bit dissed.

"He can't do both," Tony Dimes said, "I suppose."

"A simpleton," Sasha said. "Twice wrong from the start."

"What d'you write?" said Dimes. White-haired, with an unlined face, dressed in pale blue slacks and a pinkish, buttoned-down, short-sleeved shirt, he reclined on one elbow, gave off a strong scent of cologne.

"I don't know," Jeff said. "Stories. Poems. A novel, I guess. Maybe a play. I have ideas, but I don't know how to get at them. Or what to put them in."

"A bassinet," said Sasha.

"I think he's a bit stupid," Dimes said.

Sasha belched without enthusiasm, tipped up his empty glass, examined it reproachfully, screwed it into the sand.

Tony Dimes said, "You know, I think he's got something."

"Contagious?" Sasha said.

"No, no," Dimes murmured, "something physical."

"Oh," said Sasha with half a laugh.

"Too bad he's so stupid," Dimes said.

"May be an advantage," Sasha said, sounding morose.

"Your ideas?" Dimes pressed. "Name one."

"Original sin," said Jeff, for lack of better.

"We call that birth," Dimes said mildly. "But your specific subject, your donnée, as Henry James so relentlessly called it. Your mise-en-scène. What exactly?"

Jeff said, "Legless soldiers coming back from Vietnam."

"Old hat," said Sasha, perking up a bit, "unless it's agitprop. Not much room there, pretty close quarters with Hemingway, and he doesn't like company. Anyway, the real action now's in D.C. How's your Pentagon?"

"Guess I don't have one yet," Jeff allowed.

"All the same," said Dimes, "will it be a great book?"

"I doubt it," Jeff allowed.

"What a skewed point of view!" Dimes cried. "Why not?"

"Screwed," said Sabrina decisively.

"Well, the odds. . . ." Jeff said.

"An actuary," Sasha said.

"Mostly because I," said Jeff, suddenly aware that he had become light-headed, "lack vision, will, stamina, and grace."

Sighed Dimes, "He aspires to pomposity."

"Worse methods," Sasha muttered. "Would you?" Without looking he held out his glass to Sabrina, who took it and went.

"Why have you left talent off your list?" Dimes inquired.

"I haven't," said Jeff. "That's grace."

"Nonsense," Tony said with impatience. "One way or another it must be won."

Jeff felt outmaneuvered. "It depends on your theology."

"You may hope or not," Dimes said. "'Happiness is hope,' according to Dr. Johnson, of dictionary fame."

"I know who he is," Jeff said shortly.

"Was," said Tony Dimes. "With or without you must go on."

"Balls," said Sasha. "I have published how many novels? And only the first was worth a fuck."

"*Is!*" Dimes said with odd vehemence. "Ignored, perhaps, incompletely forgotten. But *is* by the few who read it cover to cover, most unpleasant. He's a magnifico. *The Breach* had a run at notoriety. Trench warfare, entirely cribbed from film, reportage, and pure invention, ends with a close-up of an immense howitzer crater of soldier parts, like a vast, ragged sunflower with a single minute woman gawking over the edge.

"His art, he used to say, meant to surpass all human vileness. He personally never sampled war. An outrage to some, sheer perversion to others. His first two, which came last, were fantastic yarns out of his own life, a wild life, one might submit—dreamers, desperadoes, billionaires, scum and scheming women. He's a maestro of nastiness—normality, he calls it. A kind of romp in the muck of ego, one critic called them. Folly triumphant. Most bracing for strong stomachs. But those are playthings beside *The Breach*. Which stymied his film career before it ever got started. An extremist in all things, he's no one's cup of tea really."

Sabrina returned on the run. Sasha like a blind solipsist took the glass from her hand, drank it down, screwed the glass back into the sand, and resumed rocking.

"Stamina is what you need," Dimes interposed with perfect complacence. "Don't get attached to anything, except life. Keep your distance. Distance is clarity. Clarity is selfless. Love art, never yourself. Keep a clean conscience, avoid regrets. Caveat emptor, especially of yourself. Don't traffic in scatology. And whatever you do, don't get married till your dotage, when nurse and secretary are essential. Wedlock is absolutely fatal, unless you're an incorrigible drunk, like Sasha here, when it's hibernation. . . ."

"Worse states," Sasha said.

"Worst of all," Dimes averred. "I'd never get a word written if I had a wife and brats, or even a lot of friends. Look at Sasha here. How's it coming, by the way?"

"Done already," Sasha muttered. "And I haven't begun."

"He'll give us another masterpiece someday, once he finds something sufficiently despicable that he knows absolutely nothing about," Dimes told Jeff, who was paying strict attention. "He needs a new virginity. My goodness! Look who's here! Hello, Millie."

"So you want to be a writer, eh?" hoarsely crowed a haggard apparition in a voluminous muumuu-like dress with egg-shaped green beads—who, having collapsed in the sand, smote Jeff on the back with her ham of a hand and then glowered in his face. "I write the best goddamned flower column you ever read," she roared. "Want to be a writer, eh? Good for you. We're the best. Painters, what d'they know? We're the ones that get the words out. Where would the world be? What d'you think happens when I've got a horrendous hangover and a goddamned deadline to meet?" She walloped Jeff on the back again. "I meet the goddamned deadline."

"Millie, you old souse, you're drunk as a coot," Sasha said.

"You're goddamned right!" she hollered. "I was a prisoner on Corregidor, the Japs let me tend their gardens, and I've been writing about flowers ever since. We won the war, I became a Buddhist, I kid you not"—she wagged a finger in Jeff's face—"the world went to hell again, as usual, and now I've got to pee."

She got up with some effort, wobbled a little way into the darkness, gathered her dress, and squatted. "We're the best!" she shouted over her whiz-whishing waters, "and don't you forget it!"

After a moment, with an effort, Sasha hoisted himself to his feet and looked around in stolid abandonment. Finally he said to Jeff, "Do you wrestle?"

Jeff shook his head, wondering how to take this.

"Don't wrestle?" Sasha said sadly. "How old do you think I am?"

Jeff figured fifty. "Sixty," he said.

"That's right," Sasha said to the sky, "sixty-six, but I'm strong as a lion...." He began to tilt, apparently unawares, but at the last moment he took a step to his left and a gulp from the refilled glass panting Sabrina had just brought on the run.

Tony Dimes said, "I used to match you drink for drink...."

"Balls," said Sasha.

"But I never got up," Dimes said.

"I can drink..." Sasha said, lost his thread, and then muttered with dire promise, "I can and will drink the whole pack of you peons into your due oblivion."

"Ode to omnipotence," Dimes murmured.

"Sasha, come and sit down," Sabrina begged, patting the sand beside her.

"Sasha, sit down," the giant minced. "Sasha, don't swim in the undertow, stop drinking so much, stop making a fool of yourself. I'll tell you one thing, Tony—if a man can't make a fool of himself he can't do anything. You're right about women, too. They won't let a man go to hell in his own way, he's got to do it *their* way. And nothing in God's green garden heats their diabolical twats like what they take to be human frailty ... frailty, my God!"

No one spoke. The silence grew long, seemed to fix the figures gathered there still as statuary. Suddenly the air filled with nearly invisible insects. Sasha brushed at his face and sat—more like fell— back on his elbows in the sand.

Bitten in several places, Jeff flailed like a windmill.

"The gnats that did in Dick Dooley," said Tony Dimes.

"Who was he?" Sabrina slapped at her knees, arms, face, where black specks alighted.

"He was here one night—murky like this one, as I recall," Dimes said. "He wandered off and wasn't seen again till next fall—his bones, that is, beautifully polished and bleached. A truly atrocious poet named Marvin Mankin took them home and strung them above his deck like a mobile. He said that in a breeze they conversed, though a bit too proverbially for his taste. He's dead, too. What became of Dooley's relics I fear we'll never know. Though they must be around here somewhere."

"You're joking," Sabrina said.

"Not at all," said Dimes. "Invariably someone perishes at Sasha's parties. It's a tradition, a ritual sacrifice, so the rest of us can go on."

"On where?" Jeff yelled, flailing.

"Wherever you're going," Dimes said.

Eddie came reeling out of the dark. "What are these bugs?"

"Ignore them," Sasha said irritably, "or get back where you belong."

"Sasha," said Dimes, "is one who won't take aspirin for a hangover."

"I love my little gnats," Sasha said.

"And they love you," said Dimes, apparently immune to them.

Sasha shivered, blinking, then sat still, hands folded in his lap. While gnats gathered on his face, he stared with challenge at Jeff, who stared back, loath to lose this test of self-mastery, initiation, endurance, whatever it might prove to be.

"Won't be a mark on him tomorrow," yawned Tony like a mind reader. "But you...."

Jeff was about to ask the brand of his cologne when a pervasive vibration in his ear all at once gained actuality like myriad tiny voices shrieking, and the hordes came. Jeff, Eddie, and Sabrina fled for the house, sped by a shout from Sasha.

Within was so crowded one could hardly move except with the general flux, which carried Eddie and Sabrina away and forced Jeff irresistibly toward the middle, while others, trying to change vantages, made him move, too. Everyone was talking vehemently without cease but of what Jeff could not make out, nor did anyone deign to notice him, much less enlighten him, till he began to feel a faint, persistent elbow in his solar plexus and managed to twist enough to discover the peevish, curling upper lip and exasperated eye of an obvious nonagenarian of parchment-like visage, who was repeating, "*Will* you kindly relieve me of this?"

A glowing nugget in the minuscule bowl of a long-stemmed pipe materialized; Jeff managed to clamp the pipe in his teeth and greedily sucked sweet hashish tinctured with opium until he coughed the world away and heard, "If you *don't* mind," and saw the pipe float off in a disembodied hand.

He kept craning his neck in the crush, hoping for another bump with Sabrina, but even had he spied her it was impossible to resist, much less steer oneself in, the social flow, as if the whole mass were one intricate organism of innumerable painted, pinioned buoys bobbing in a choppy sea, and he none the wiser for all the tireless talk that flew past like spindrift.

"'Tell him you shit on him from a great elevation," said a familiar voice. "That's what your father always said to me when he was annoyed."

"Did he?" said a boy with golden curls.

"Frequently."

"Something's going on behind all this," Jeff said. "One day we'll wake up and everything will be different."

"You're blithering," Sabrina cried, hugging him.

"Who's this guy, Sasha?" he asked, trying to keep an arm around her, but quick she slipped away.

"He's my stepfather," the boy said. "I'm George. I just came home tonight. I've never read a word of his horrid oeuvre, and I never will."

"I'm so high I could fly or die and never know the difference," Sabrina said.

"I think it's perfectly charming," remarked Tony Dimes.

"It's too long," Sasha said. "It turns him into a girl."

"Very seductive," said Tony. "I advise you not to cut one lock of it."

George, graceful and slender, smiled composedly down at the two men who were still sitting in the sand. The gnats were gone, though Jeff, who noticed he was back in the sand himself, wasn't sure he hadn't imagined them, nor did he know how he'd gotten there, or if he'd actually entered the little toy house. He felt a need to get a grip on things, find an empty space to rest and take stock.

"You'd better have it cut by noon tomorrow," Sasha said.

"I shit on you from a great elevation," said George.

Sasha sat still as if vacant or deep in contemplation.

"I shit on you from an even greater elevation," George said with languid prep-school precision.

"Insults! From everyone. Even the whelp of my whore," Sasha said heavily. "Now you must wrestle."

"I've been waiting for you to say that ever since I arrived," said George.

"Bravo!" cried Tony Dimes. "Up with you both! Everyone's got a purchase on something. Jeff here's a theologian. Sasha's the last lion. George . . . George will slay women, I predict. Or men. Or both. Mascot Sabrina beggars prophecy." He leaned back on his elbow.

"Oh, Tony," Sabrina cried, "I do adore you, you're such a fey uncle."

Snorting, Sasha rose with difficulty and half-bent as George darted at his ankles. "Whelp of my whore," Sasha said, fending him off with a casual hand. They locked arms, broke off, locked again. George slipped free, grabbed one arm, yanked Sasha forward, kicked a foot from under him, stepped behind, and gave such a push to his trajectory that he went flying flat on his face. George pinned him with a hammerlock. There was no sound but Sasha's loud gasping.

Jeff stood up, appalled.

"A sham," said Dimes. "What a sham."

Sasha, who now seemed to be napping, with a sudden grunt heaved himself up, thrust the boy above his head, and hurled him into the sand, where he lay as though dead.

"Still champion of the sand pit," Dimes intoned with mild derision.

George rose to one knee, shaking the sand from his hair, accepting his defeat with grace as if he cared not one jot, but Sasha shadow-boxed in a circle, darting punches. "Come on," he said to Tony. "One hand behind my back."

"You know I never get up," Tony said.

"You?" Sasha said with mock menace to Jeff, who sat back down.

"You're missing an immortal flight," George advised him.

"I want someone real to wrestle with," Sasha said dismally. "Hey," he shouted at the house. "Come out here, one of you eunuchs, and give me a round." When no one answered—all appeared accustomed to his antics—he made several disconsolate turns like a top running down, dropped to his knees, put his head back, and howled.

The sound went up in the dead, airless heat. No one spoke. Sasha howled, more and more forlorn, preposterous, buffoonish, but still succeeding by some aura beyond abasement in affirming that all this was but a fantastic charade flung at his guests by one who, notwithstanding his apparent disarray, had once done fine things, and held yet finer things in sway.

All stopped with Sasha winded, hoarse-panting. Finally, after several precarious efforts, he regained his feet and listed unsteadily toward the house, then seemed to think again, hung his head, and veered back toward the path.

"Sasha," a woman's voice called, "Sasha, where are you going?"

"A little drive," he panted.

"Why?" the woman said. "Where?"

"For no reason," Sasha said. "Nowhere."

"We'll be having breakfast soon. We need you to make the omelets. Please, Sasha. George is going to help, he came home especially. You could take a little nap before."

"What should I want with a nap?"

"Please," the woman said. "Oh, Sasha, please."

"I want to take a little drive," he muttered. "Clear my head."

"May I come?" Sabrina said with a caressive plea.

"No, no," he said. "Not this time."

"You promised," she said. "Remember?"

"Always, my dear, and this once more." He seemed to pause, almost to recant, but then finally touched her cheek and started up the path, one step at a time, as if he knew it might take all night.

"When was the last time he fit himself into that car?" Tony Dimes said. "He'll come rolling back down at dawn like a barrel of monkeys."

Sabrina looked about to cry, opened her mouth, shut it wordless.

Sasha was a dim shadow rising in the dark, stopping to rest, then going up, interminably up, while they waited in various guises of curiosity. He finally appeared at the top and raised one hand—in a wave or reach for balance—and went from sight.

They sat in silence, caught in thought. Little by little they emerged from the moment. The muffled rumble of an engine coming to life occupied them again. Headlights crossed the sky and vanished.

"Entertainment over. Bedtime for me," sang Dimes, cheerful and brisk. He rose to his feet, lithe as a boy. "Good luck," he said, dropping eerily long, thin, soft, dry fingertips down to Jeff. "Goodbye, goodbye. Keep the faith, all. Unless you'd care to come? I'm not averse to a nightcap."

Whom he addressed was unclear—perhaps it was mere whimsy.

"The chef too must go," said George after a moment. "I've got to do some prep. Sasha likes things done just so. Otherwise I'll have to wrestle again. Such a bore."

"Someday you'll win," said Dimes.

"I don't know," George said. "I'm not holding my breath. I hope not."

Oppressed, Jeff went in search of Eddie and found him behind the house, embracing a woman, who slipped back inside. "It's four thirty," Jeff said.

"Well, I guess," said Eddie.

They went back to take leave of Sabrina. "Oh, no, I'm coming too," she said.

"No omelet?" said Jeff.

"I loathe eggs," she said. At the summit she kicked at the sports car's sheath, slumped there like a parachute or the panties of a giantess.

It seemed an interminable jouncing, bouncing rattle of being tossed against each other till at last they turned onto the empty highway. "George invited me to go horseback riding with him on the beach tomorrow at midnight," Sabrina said. "It's low tide and full moon."

"Accounts for all that howling," Jeff said, trying to shim his fingers under her.

"I've always wanted to be the mistress of a father and son at the same time," she said.

"Stepson," said Jeff.

She bit him on the shoulder so hard he heard her teeth crunch.

He tried to hit her with his free elbow, but she caught his wrist. "I've got rabies," she said. "You better see a doctor. And keep your hands off me, I don't want your bloody hands on me. You're repulsive."

Jeff began to scream with rage, but she pulled his far hand between her thighs, moaning, "Oh, honey, I'm so horny, I didn't mean to hurt you," tilting her bottom, letting his other hand have its way, which calmed him instantly. He took a deep breath, then another, and another.

The gashed flesh dulled as his finger pads met slick entrance. He briefly bereaved one hand to snap on the light, with the intent to get Eddie to check how bad the bite was, but Eddie was too preoccupied to look.

In front of them, far down a long flat, floating toward them in the headlights of a stopped pickup truck, was something beyond intelligible. They bore down on it beneath their overhead light in ghostly silence.

Something had hit a parked bulldozer. Sighing, Eddie pulled up behind the truck. After a mute moment they got out, stood transfixed.

"Like a squashed can," Eddie said.

A boy in clean coveralls came to meet them. He stopped at some distance to say, "I hope it's no one you know."

Sabrina, holding her face in both hands, threw up an astounding puddle.

They backed away in haste. Looking queasy, the boy said, "I have to go. I'm sorry."

Jeff called after him, "Are you sure. . . ?"

"See for yourself," the boy said, getting into his truck. Once on the road he gunned it.

When the sound had faded Jeff forced himself to approach tentatively, as if it might be a sleeping beast. His eyes cleared, told him there could be no doubt, and he turned back.

He shook his head at Sabrina, who opened her mouth to scream, but no sound came out.

Eddie stayed with the wreck. Jeff made a U-turn in the empty road, his shoulder pulsating.

"What a fool," he said. "He fell asleep at the wheel."

"That was no accident," Sabrina said.

Jeff felt his face grimacing. "Won his own argument," he said.

Sabrina said, "His new book was almost done. He's been working on it for years. Years and years. Why would he do this?"

"Maybe he didn't like this one any better than the others."

"Everybody liked his first one best. Godawful as it was."

In the mirror Jeff glimpsed a strange pair of staring eyes. He snapped off the light. "How long was that bulldozer there?"

"Oh, he'd have found something," she said in a dull voice.

The rattling van rattled and rattled.

"He's the only man I ever really loved," she said as they turned off the old road onto the track into the dunes. She bent double, rocking in her seat.

Jeff glanced at her in bafflement. It hadn't occurred to him that death might come in any form but time, unless in Vietnam.

Sabrina said, "He never fucked me even once. He said he loved me but he was always so distracted. He had so many lovers, famous, beautiful ones."

Jeff put his hand in her hair for a moment.

When they reached the top she was out of the van before he'd gotten parked, stumbling to her knees, then striding for the pit. He followed slowly, privately, in stately procession.

Halfway down he stood aside for a woman going up, raging, Sabrina choking behind.

When he reached the bottom he took the first bottle that came to hand, walked out beyond the lights, and sat in the sand, gazing at the house where the party seemed in desultory exodus. He drank sadly and bravely, mourning for Sasha, wondering what sort of commemoration could follow. First, he would try to find a copy of *The Breach*—the least he could do, "quick as the Lord would let him," in the parlance of a favorite late uncle's most urgent admonition.

He must have dozed or dreamt. He ached from head to toe, as if he'd been in a cement mixer. Time had gone awry. The little house was dark, the doors shut; the sky was alight, the sun flaring on the walls' blackened rim.

He got to his feet with difficulty, lurched in a circle, and then sank back down to rest. He could see no path, only thousands and thousands of footprints all the same, like minuscule vales, leading nowhere.

.

for Eddie Ritter
History doesn't repeat itself, but it rhymes, it rhymes.
—attributed to Mark Twain

Noon in the Old Colony Tap, 2005

◇◇◇◇◇◇◇◇◇◇◇◇◇◇◇◇◇◇◇◇◇◇◇◇◇◇◇◇

Yeah, every once in a while you gotta get a little taste of the good stuff, have a cigarette, cup of coffee—whatever makes the world look good even for a minute, change your perspective. Sit here, look out the window—all those people going by, they have no idea what's happening, they're just down for the weekend. They have weekends, these people. Clothes, fancy cars, you name it. Well, good luck to them. I don't want anything they've got. I wouldn't want to be in their shoes either.

Yeah, you gotta have a little lift once in a while, a little spark. Doesn't last long though. Then you've got to step right back into it. I might like a Jameson, but I can't, I can't do it. Those days are long gone.

I'll tell ya, there's a lotta hardship out there. No one knows unless you're in it. There's no jobs. No fish. Vets I know—you wouldn't believe what goes on—all of a sudden they put in for mental disability, trauma counseling and all that. I'd rather eat out of garbage cans. You know what I mean?

Well, we got rid of Saddam, but I don't think it was worth it. What's the toll now? Over a thousand? They only count the dead, never mind the wounded—guys, terrible wounds, they'll be ruined all their lives, just kids some of them, hands, legs, feet missing, ears burnt off, blind, guts shot out, so scarred you can't even look at them. Walking around with urine bags.

Yeah, everything's going good, going great. You see that, Cheney? Some day we'll wake up. Like with Vietnam. How come we forgot all that?

When I got out in '68 I had a real hard time. I was crazy. I didn't care what happened to me. I saw too much, things I never told anyone. American dead: 58,000.

That's a big number. Ever hear the number wounded? How about civilians, women and babies? What number would that be? That's one they don't let out, that's one nobody wants to hear.

I was in jail for sixty-six days. Don't ask me what I did to get there—I sunk so low I couldn't even bother to take a shit. I'd've killed myself if I had a gun, that's the truth. I was sitting on a bench in this big exercise cage. I was hunched over, elbows on my knees, head in my hands, just staring at my feet.

This Indian, this Native American, he never spoke before, he always stood off by himself, he came over, he says, "I want to tell you something my father taught me. Whatever happens, you keep your head up. Always keep your head up. Whatever happens."

I know it doesn't sound like much, but I never forgot it.

Wellll, we got to lighten up here. I'll tell you a story. I went home for a while. My mother's not doing so good. She's old, she can't get out of her chair, she can't remember anything—my name, her name, who I am, who she is, where she is, who's still alive, who's dead.

All she does is ask what time it is, and it drives us all crazy. All the time she's worrying, worrying. You can see she never gets any rest, she can't even remember what she's supposed to be worrying about, you can see her trying to figure it out—make dinner, do the laundry, lock the door and windows, are us kids home from school?—but she can't make anything out of it. It's all a fog except What time is it? What time is it? And it doesn't matter what we say. Sometimes we go backwards, to keep from going buggy ourselves.

So I thought—I've got to try something, I can't just leave her like this. I bought a book of nursery rhymes, like she used to read to us.

And she remembered all the rhymes. I'd read right up to a rhyme and stop, and she'd say the rhyme. We couldn't believe it.

I'd say, Little Jack Horner sat in a ... and she'd say *corner*. Twinkle, twinkle, little star, how I wonder what you ... *are*. She remembered all the rhymes, every one. It was hilarious. My brother was rolling on the floor in hysterics.

Then she wanted me to tell her a story. I says, Ma, I can't tell you a story.

She says, Tell me a story about fishing.

My brother says, Yeah, come on. You can. That's the one thing you can do.

So, I didn't know—then I thought of this big flounder I caught. So I said, There was this starving fisherman and his wife, and they lived in a shack. One day he caught this huge flounder. I mean HUGE. It was so big and beautiful he didn't want to kill it, so he let it go.

His wife wakes up in the middle of the night. She jabs him in the ribs with her elbow, she says, Are you kidding? We got to eat. Go back and see if you can catch it again.

So he gets out of bed and rows out and catches the fish again, but this time the flounder says, I'm a prince.

So naturally he lets it go. His wife, she doesn't know what to say. They go back to sleep. She wakes up about four a.m. Jabs him in the ribs. You didn't ask for a boon? You're supposed to ask for a boon for letting it go.

So next day same thing, he rows out, catches the flounder. He begs a boon. He says, Ohhh, maybe a nice house for my wife.

Gets home. Beautiful house, his wife's in the kitchen singing. Oh, yeah, and food, too, steak and all the latest appliances, you name it. Middle of the night she jabs him with her elbow. Go catch that flounder again. I want a castle.

Next day he goes back, he tells the flounder, A castle for my wife, please.

Gets home, there she is. Queen in her castle.

But she's been thinking. Middle of the night she jabs him in his sore rib. I want my own country.

Same thing, he gets home, everything's perfect, the size of our old neighborhood in Brooklyn, only it's trees with birds, horses and cows drinking out of a nice, cool pond, lots of trout, no troubles though. Only happy people.

Next day she decides she wants to be president, no problem. He doesn't even have to catch the flounder—it jumps into his boat like a trained seal. But that doesn't turn out so hot, too many nasty looks. So then she says, I want to be the pope.

The fisherman thinks that might be a bit much, being a Catholic and all. Of course Ma's never missed a Sunday.

But. He walks down to the water, has a word with the flounder, gets home, and she's all in a white cassock with gold trim, looks like a million bucks. Pope? she says. Why pope? Why are we wasting all this time? Tell the flounder I want to be God. And then I'll put things right.

The fisherman is kind of scared to ask for that. Maybe he's embarrassed to keep bugging the flounder after it has already been so nice, but whatever his wife wants, that's okay with him. So he hems and haws and then very tactfully he hints that his wife would like to be God, and the flounder stands up on its tail and salutes, and then it slides down into the sea very slowly, big as the sun.

The fisherman gets home and what does he find? What d'you think he found?

I said, Come on, Ma, you know. I know you know. You know the answer to this one, I know you do. It's like a riddle. You know the answer.

She just sat there smiling, I could see her trying, but she just couldn't do it. You know, Ma. Yes, you do. I know you do. I kept coaxing. She's like a little kid, she knows she knows, but she can't get it out.

Yeah, I says. You guessed it. I know you did. You knew all along. I know you know.

All she could do was smile. Finally I had to give up. I had to say it for her—Everything's right back where it started from. They're back in their shack with a little tiny minnow on the table.

Ma clapped her hands together and rocked in her chair, she was so happy. We all got a good laugh out of that.

for Michael Burkard

Nothing Happens Again

◇◇◇◇◇◇◇◇◇◇◇◇◇◇◇◇◇◇◇◇◇◇◇

The year was almost gone. Spring was surging. April 30 loomed like a kind of tombstone, marking the season when birds shit copious purple from eating ivy berries, splotching steps and windshields, and the Fine Arts Work Center Fellows prepare to leave—a period naturally frenzied, sad, apprehensive, uncertain, dazed by sun after winter's raw chill.

They had gone to the Old Colony because the Fo'c'sle was full of oafs and they wanted to enjoy themselves together, perhaps for the last time.

Elsie was a poet, Joanna a fiction writer; Bea and Astrid were painters; Chantel was the wife of one of the writing Fellows, a novelist herself and rejected applicant. They were embarking upon careers unlikely to provide lasting addresses till who knew when? But for the moment all were at home, all had great hopes and great thirsts.

"We should have done this more often," said Joanna. "When we had the chance. What a day."

They marveled at the balmy weather, which brought out hibernators and hermits alike. Astrid described a guy she'd met on the meat rack whose right arm was a withered stump, the result of his doctor's drunken malpractice.

The guy had been grandly casual about it, gesturing with his left hand.

Astrid quoted, "'I got his license, I'm going to get his house, I'm going to get his car, I'm going to get his bank account—I'm going to get everything he's got. I don't have any hard feelings. I just don't want him to have anything.'"

"I don't blame him," said Joanna, glancing both ways warily over her glass and then ducking a bit to sip. "Did you read in the *Globe* about Charles Boyer's death after he sat this long vigil with his wife who was dying of cancer? He kept assuring her she was going to recover. Meanwhile he was putting off a prostate operation. He wasted away at her bedside, and then when she died he committed suicide."

"I like that one better," said Elsie.

Bea said, "My mother is demanding I come home and take care of my sick grandmother—*her* mother—who took care of *me* when she wouldn't."

Chantel said, "Don't do it."

"How can I not do it?" Bea said. "She'll just abandon her, like she abandoned me."

"You said you were going to Yaddo," Astrid accused her.

"I was," Bea said.

"Yeah," Astrid said with resigned disgust.

"You only have one life," Joanna put in ruefully.

"Old age is pathetic," Elsie pursued. "A woman I know—she's probably seventy—she hired a girl to look after her ninety-year-old mother, who's senile. The girl's about fifteen, totally innocent and terribly upset. Between diaper changes, she tried to restore the mother's mind by making her do mental exercises, like relearn the alphabet and add and subtract. The poor woman can't bear to disillusion the girl, but she doesn't want her mother bothered either."

"Why should it bother her?" Astrid crowed. "Hey, she's out of it!"

"I think I'll draw the line at diapers," Bea said tartly.

"How did we get to be so morbid all of a sudden?" said Elsie.

"Yeah," Joanna agreed with amazed vehemence. "We're supposed to be having a good time."

"Have you noticed," asked Chantel, "how many people seem to be changing their names these days?"

"Who?" Astrid said. "Why?"

"A lot of people," said Chantel, about to theorize when Claire came in disheveled and distraught.

"I looked in the Fo'c'sle for you," she said. "Have you heard?"

"Heard what?" they all said together.

"Eleanor Crimins got killed," Claire said. "In a car crash. Up in Vermont. Borrowing her brother's van. The office got a call. They said you'd all gone drinking."

"So we had," Chantel murmured.

Eleanor Crimins was everybody's confidante, a wise, even-tempered, good painter on the verge of success.

Claire sat down at the window table with them. They gaped at her with horrid shock, the dead woman's colleagues—Elsie, the intense, with square bangs and frown furrows already deeply graven between her eyes, quick to anger, quick to laugh; Irish Joanna, tall and slender, hesitant, with quavers in her voice, indignant at injustice, lately bedeviled by too many lovers; blond Bea from Pine Bluff, Arkansas, the only one in a skirt, complacent and edgy, whose secretly written novel was nearing completion; raucous, sarcastic Astrid, who smoked dope all day at her easel and dressed in thrift-shop getups; pale, sylphlike Chantel, with her porcelain complexion, ash-blond hair, and startling, Bay of Naples blue eyes, a withdrawn, watchful chain-smoker.

Divorced, manic-depressive Claire, in career the most advanced, two years ago a featured poet of the *Benedict Review*, had written nothing since but some scattered notes, her long allure lost to flotsam and collage, her days to agonized debility, dreamy beachcombing.

"I don't know," she kept answering their one question. "I think she was on a picnic or something. The road was strewn with sandwiches and soft drinks and stuff, carrot sticks and celery, they said."

"I don't believe it," Astrid cried, her voice flying up. "I just don't believe it. How old was she?"

"Thirty-one," Elsie said.

"Beats me by two years," said Astrid, to whom the specter of death was a daily visitant. She was the oldest of them except Claire, who was thirty-three.

Joanna said, "I don't believe it either. I can't stand to think about it. About her, I mean."

"Is her mother still alive?" Bea asked.

Yes, yes, the others nodded.

"This is terrible," Elsie said. "This is the worst thing I ever heard. Or had happen. My first friend to die."

"She was a terrific painter," Astrid said. "How could this happen?"

Two cars on a highway. Smash. What were the odds? It would never happen to you. Blank sorrow ruled. Eyes were drenched; hugs bent till they hurt; incoherence gnashed in its depths.

Pausing, panting, they drank.

"Well," Astrid said at last, lifting her mug, "I suppose we should ... Here's to her."

They drank.

"I have a feeling I'm not going to feel the same about things after this is over," Joanna said direly.

Chantel said, "It doesn't get over."

"I refuse to believe this," Bea said. "I really feel as if I could will her back to life."

"We should try," said Elsie. "All together."

Holding hands, eyes battened shut, they tried to bring Eleanor Crimins back from death, undo the done; presently they breathed again, drank. Chantel lighted a new cigarette. Astrid, who'd quit smoking, took one, too.

"I'm getting sick to my stomach," Joanna said.

"I am sick to my stomach," Claire said.

"She's dead," Elsie said. "She's actually dead."

"Don't remind me," Astrid said.

"I walked to the post office with her," Bea said, "day before yesterday."

Everybody but Claire, who lived off Center, had seen her, had spoken with her. They'd all been out in the sun.

"Yeah," Astrid said. "She was feeling pretty good. She said she was over her depression."

"This is one of those really amazing things," Claire said, "that you don't want to have happen."

"God has a plan," Bea railed dully.

"No show for Eleanor," said Astrid.

"That's right!" Elsie cried. "She was going to have a show in August. In Boston."

"She can still have it," said Bea.

"Great," Astrid groaned with leaden irony then, "yeah. Well. She should. We ought to have something down here, too. At the Work Center." For a little minute minds in accord were occupied with plans, dates, logistics.

Desolation came again. Astrid and Bea made their shrunken way to the bar with empty mugs and brought back another round.

Gone. Forever. Food for worms. Or fire. Future cancelled. Past annulled. The late Eleanor Crimins.

"I think I've got to go throw up. Excuse me," Joanna said, rising in haste.

Long-faced Chantel sat in silent thought, chin in one hand, tall tendril of smoke rising from the other. She might have been anywhere, anytime, for the fixed look of her, eyes downcast like half-moons, a totem brooding.

Bea wore a scowl none of them had ever seen before. "This is not right," she said.

"Nothing's right," Elsie said.

"I know," Bea said.

"I think I expected to know her all my life," Astrid marveled.

"And she was just getting going. I love her new paintings," Joanna said, returning. Then, to their eyes, she said, "I feel better. Not much."

"Yeah. A piece of our lives just...." Elsie opened her palms, emptied them up.

"This is horrifying," Astrid said. "I can't take it."

Mute fatality, bellies' yaw and fall, thud of tidal blood, each breath a sigh or moan.

At last Claire cried, "I can't help it—I wish I'd never told you."

They shook their heads. Not your fault. Better to learn like this than one by one, alone.

Radley, heading for the Fo'c'sle from the West End, having penned an unprecedented thirty lines in one day, spied them in the window, went jovially in. "Witches' coven?" said he.

All looked at him, stark, waiting for another to speak.

"CR group?" he tried, more snidely.

They looked at him with dire woe, without personal expression.

He read there some onerous kind of unwelcome, held up two fingers of his left hand, waggled them twice in blessing, backed up, and went out the door, turned by the window, eyes averted.

"Who wants to tell anybody," Astrid said. "He'll find out soon enough."

"Where is he? Her ex, I guess," Bea asked. "Mr. Trouble."

"Tucson," Elsie said shortly.

"Let the office make that call," Claire said.

"He got out in the nick of time," Astrid said.

"That's right," Bea said. "He might have been with Eleanor. Be with her right now. In the morgue."

"Sleazeball," Elsie said.

"What d'you mean, sleazeball?" Joanna said. "He was nice. I liked him."

"You like everybody," Astrid said.

Joanna puffed out her lower lip, dropped her chin with rue, and said, "I guess you're right about that."

Glancing left and right, Joyce sauntered down the street from the east and came in. She looked at them cheerily. "Why aren't you in the Fo'c'sle? Everybody's there."

They looked at her in horrified consternation.

Joyce said, "Don't worry, don't worry, it's all a mistake. Somebody borrowed her brother's van. He wasn't hurt, but there was a whole family of Canadians in the other car. Three dead, three in the hospital. What she called to say was she wouldn't be coming back till she could find another van, but the person who took the call is a new volunteer who doesn't know anyone. I guess Eleanor was pretty upset." Dumbfounded joy erupted.

"Wish I always brought such good news," said Joyce, whose gallery in town had just given her a bad slot in early June, when nothing would sell. "Feeling better, dears?" she said, and grinned wickedly.

"You can't even imagine," Astrid shouted over the laughter and tears.

"I'll bet," said Joyce, broadening her grin. "That would have made this a pretty grim day. How old is she anyway? She's having a show, isn't she?"

"Oh, I'm going to go," Astrid said, all admonishment.

Oh, yes, they'd all be at the opening, with bells on and ringing. . . .

Their voices spiraled louder and louder, laughing, crying, and yelling all at once, reliving what they had felt and thought, rejoicing.

Joanna's face had turned bright red; she grinned wildly, speechlessly, uncontrollably. Elsie was laughing without pause for breath, the frown lines cutting deep between her eyes. Astrid and Bea had gotten shots of Bushmills to help them calm down and celebrate in peace.

Claire, dazed between wonder and doubt, headed back to the Work Center to check and recheck the facts of what had happened at a certain crossroads up in Vermont, where winter's icy writ still ran.

Joyce, who had no use for alcohol, glanced from one to another curiously, fondly, amused and touched, made mocking comment when chance offered.

A placid ribbon of blue smoke, doubling upon itself, rose from Chantel's fresh cigarette where she sat apart, silent and pale, elbow propped on crossed knee, chin in hand, bent forward as if in duress about whether to get up and go elsewhere or remain as she was, staring out the window at the empty street, immune to relief, the whole nub of things unchanged, while their lives began to possess them again.

Pills

◇◇◇◇

ozma Volkov leaned in the doorway of the sunny summer kitchen, bent in disbelief, mystified, mortified, aghast at the sabotage of his own carefully planned suicide. Where was it, that saving vial so cunningly, so—he winced to recall—so gratifyingly concealed in his cavernous, cluttered barn studio largely abandoned these last two years, except for when he watched TV, or when he sat dozing or reading in his shabby armchair, a studio where his wife, Varvara Aronovna, hadn't set foot in ages.

"It's wall-to-wall booby traps," she once confided to an interviewer with perfect complacence. He himself could sleepwalk its serpentine ways in the dark dead drunk, and how not? He'd spent the last fifty years there, now painted en plein air only in high summer.

But why had he felt such need to hide those pills? She didn't rummage or snoop. And where? Where? Where could he have put what had afforded him such comfort, such solace, such certainty of surcease, this whole, last, grisly epoch of ill health and humiliating decline? It had not been easy to suborn his old pal, Dr. Bones, up in Boston, but bless him for a friend indeed, possessor of two, no, three of Kozma's paintings.

"Thank you, Josip," he said aloud, hoping no dread had ensued, or still impended. He would have liked to phone about this moment's gratitude, but he couldn't, not at this date, those thanks anyway long since most earnestly manifested. So many things he would no longer fuss about. Eventually everything, and soon, quite soon, today. In fact, tonight.

Sworn, bound to his timely terminus, he must be done with it by this hour tomorrow, when Vara returned to read his revised farewell, announcing his permanent disappearance—*if* he could contrive it—unspeakable reunion, if not. Loathsome the thought of her finding him still here, still breathing. Comedy of all comedies, to fail at suicide. Now pill-less, he must improvise. He thought first of gun convenience, the irreversible trigger-jerk, no margin for change of mind or faintness of heart, but bullets were inconsiderately messy, and he had no gun, knew no way to get one, hated them anyway. Amateur hanging—what horrid gurglings to die by, bulging eyeballs to greet her, repulsive swan song.

He balled and burned the original page, composed anew, repeating his hopes that she had enjoyed her little jaunt and visit with friends in Ithaca, then redoubled apologies for his desertion.

The original letter had consigned his corpse—too vivid, replaced with *remains*, then *body*, finally *me*—to the crematorium, grim destination, now no longer his.

The new farewell extolled concession, withdrawal, silence.

She need not, she should not seek. He was gone whence he had come, which was nowhere—not quite exact, of course, but metaphorically, metaphysically accurate. He was sure she would forgive, if not dance a jig. Poor soul! How he had loved her! So long ago!

She should never, ever, he adjured her, report him missing. She might answer eventual queries—they had lived lives of virtual seclusion—by reference to the casual note he'd left (and she'd not kept) explaining that he'd gone by bus to sit with a dying friend in Maine (she had the car, he hated flying, took the ferry) but had forgotten to leave her the man's name, address, or phone. North it was, very far north, somewhere north of Presque Isle.

If Kozma hated anything more than blood, it was water—he never gave it a glance, much less drank or wasted a drop of paint on it—all the same level of instability, waves an alien bore.

Trees he had painted till they revealed their irreducible majesty, even, perhaps especially, the gnarled, misshapen locusts of Cape Cod. But water—water was the reigning medium here, that and the uncommanding sand; thus, water was the way he now must go.

So long as it got done somehow. "Vara, dear," he wrote, "I've gone to sea. Weep not, search not for me. I've taken the outbound tide, jumped off the ferry halfway to Boston."

Such, he hoped, she would accept. A feat, of course, in his decrepitude, impossible to execute—to climb the rail, drop unseen, unnoticed into the bow billow rolling away, and not keep bobbing up—no, not a chance, only wretchedness of rescue, wrapped in blanket solicitude, officious faces, farcical questions. "What made you think you wanted to die? Now, after your little dive and dip, aren't you glad you're still alive?" Not adept at wiles, Kozma was practiced in imagination. Vara should say airily, "Oh, he'll be back one of these days."

The final act of a life of art might, with no lack of propriety, provide a legacy of perfect mystery. That he would forever after always be yet to write, yet to call, yet to appear in person at his own door, would mark him, perhaps, finally, as a dilatory or even a faithless Wakefield—at least in some eyes—so much the better for beguilement of speculation, collectors, prices, sales, with harm to none, vantage only to Vara.

Aloud he vaunted his old motto, "Life is hard but art is harder." Pomposity. Cowardice. He just wanted out. Heaven it looked now, to lie down with a belly full of pills, as planned, with a glass of fine, frigid vodka in hand and the genius of Shostakovich's preludes to dance and dirge him away.

But now that simply could not be. Fantasies, comforting fantasies. At six o'clock, impossibly restive, he limped down the cellar stairs, brought up the antique portmanteau, cracked black leather and tarnished buckle, with two lead window-sash weights roped together, wrapped in a torn work shirt—from when or whose he no longer knew, if he ever had.

What *could* he remember? His present errand he wouldn't forget, perhaps that one thing only. Lucky, lucky to have been kept for years and years unknown, unthought of, thus un-thrown-out, these providential saviors, that weighed—God help him—almost more than he could lift. He paused in wretched regard of this, his stand-in for the merciful, decorous, so oddly lost, so . . . so—he could almost believe—so willfully dematerialized pills. By evening, too agitated for further search, he lugged the bag beyond sight of the house in the brutal heat, stopping to gasp for breath, rest, and change arms, praying no familiar face would spy him on the road or greet him on the bus.

Safe aboard the shuttle at last, hunched beneath a baseball cap, visor pulled down level with his ears, gaunt visage shadowed by large-rimmed dark tortoiseshell glasses, he seemed to drowse, while the rickety-rackety bus jolted and jarred, ground gears like a behemoth clearing its hoarse, massive throat, steadily filling, as people got on, got on, kept getting on, increasingly squeezed in the unheard-of humidity, suffocating compaction endured with eyes aloft and aloof.

Midtown, last stop, finally hove into view—the cram-packed municipal parking lot, bracketed by MacMillan and Cabral's Wharfs with their docks and rust-bitten draggers, crowded finger-piers and pleasure craft, the boarding and disembarking whale-watch boats, to the west the whole bay a petrified forest of motionless masts, not a breath in the solid heat, a maximum of ticketholders limply lined up, languishing for the offshore breezes, if any, to be found on the Bay Lady's evening sail.

Like an agglutinated, sweat-clung centipede, passengers inched down the aisle, avid to regain their singularities. Waited till last, Kozma Volkov stumbled on the bottom step, pitched headlong, skinned elbows, knees, forehead, got gravel ingrained in his soft palms.

"Here, let me," said a voice, helping hands under his arms, easing him up. "Good God, what's this, Fort Knox?"

"It's nothing," said Kozma.

"Nothing!" quietly cried the man with quizzical eye. "Are you going farther west? Or east? I have a car, happy to drive you."

"I'm just here," said Kozma, "for the duration."

"Well," said the man, "you could use some Mercurochrome and a few Band-Aids. You look a fright."

"I have no doubt," said Kozma.

"Ah," murmured the man, reluctant, stroking his chin. "Well. Take better care of yourself, Granddad." He reached out a hand just short of touch.

Kozma bowed. Sudden tears flooded his eyes. Violent headshakes flung them away like blown rain. When he looked up again the man was gone.

As he crossed the parking lot, tilting with the bag, he surveyed his progeny, near phantoms now deep in time—Sergei Shavrov, Captain, 1st Marine Wing, lost in the Battle of the Chosin Reservoir, December 2, 1950; Marta, estranged in Poland with grown, married twins, who inhabited a world nearly as distant as that of Vara's family, dead of the Nazis, those the Reds hadn't killed.

He sat on a bench, a small, bald, potbellied, untidy man with reticent eyes, raw bruises, and knee-torn pants, beside him the black bag, at his back the vast, traversed parking lot. He had—he could have—no complaints, only regret that his time had come, and a twinge of distaste that he could not just die, but must kill, his sole enemy, his life.

His tree-shaded bench was the middle one of nine, spaced ten feet apart, each with its canopy of foliage and unkempt shrubbery. At his feet a hundred yards of walkway connected the two great wharves. A foot-high, two-foot-wide cement safety barrier sided the walkway itself and then, as seawall, dropped straight down to a brief stretch of vacant harbor. At high tide the water would be but four or five feet below the walkway—he would slip from life straight to the bottom with hardly a splash. On a calm, cloudless day, at dead low ebb, when the tide was ten or twelve feet down, intermittent gleams of silvery things dropped or tossed in glimmered through the surface, while an orange spot of sun wobbled in the water's gently rocking motion, with an almost greeny halo—odd phenomenon, odder yet to recall it now.

From when? And would moonbeams, too, appear there to dance over his bones? No. Over his still-fleshed corpse maybe, but briefly, if all went as planned. The sky was clear, no evening star. Not yet.

It must be nearing eight—he'd left his watch, he'd left everything behind. High tide was midnight. Zero hour. He'd got here with time to spare. Spacious, his remaining span, infinitely spacious. He needn't even start on valedictories, not yet, not yet. He could go get a bottle of water, if he dared leave his window-sash weights. Who would steal them? He could lug them over to the Surf Club and have dinner, then lug them back. But he had no appetite, not even for vodka. Why should he? No call for anything but clarity, concentration, focus, no drift or dream, his wont of late.

For the moment all was mundane, fearless, with no remorse—not even for abandoning Vara. How he had loved her! How instantly wet she would get, her bum's cleft aflutter at his fingertips' first inquisitions. At love she always wept wildly while she came, hugging him so hard—her slender little self never failed to amaze, leave him in warm dreams of her. "Don't stop!" she once cried out. "Don't ever stop!"

How had he got here from there? Way of all life. No matter how hard you worked, you never, ever finished. Life by trial of ego. Canvases, canvases, canvases. Carcass. Goodbye. Don't care, can't care. Only mourn. And she too must go. All go. Where? Nowhere. Paint he loved, paint above all else.

The bay glittered like bolero played by sitar. He got up stiffly and dropped his dark glasses overboard; they had been left behind years ago, by some forgotten visitor. He sat back down again, all things done, all prepared—now only the wait was real.

Hiding at the edge of the woods till dark, a kid in rags, following a narrow, arrow-straight track, lush grass in the middle, uniform palisades of spiring pines on both sides, no branches, topped with V-like tufts, nothing else but high, white sky, then the trance of earthbound distance ahead, a black hole like a tunnel, Poland, he hoped.

German voices. In terror he peeped through the undergrowth. Two soldiers with chest-hung assault weapons were hiking along. Suddenly they stopped dead still.

Zipping his fly, coming toward them head-on, a military policeman demanded their papers: his harsh, peremptory tone for years tipped Kozma's sleep toward free-fall horror.

Not ten yards from him, the three stopped face-to-face. One of the Krauts with casual ease swung his barrel and stitched the MP from belt to chin. The other put his muzzle in the shooter's ear, blew half his head away, and walked on. For years those two bloody bodies and the one who never glanced back had spelled life to Kozma. And then he met Varvara Aronovna, who took him straight to bed.

Elbows on his knees, he sat on, picking gravel from the heels of his hands. Over his shoulder he could see the shuttle, reboarding for the East End and Beach Point. In the morning, at six thirty-three or six thirty-four, the Plymouth & Brockton bus would roar past his house on its way to North Truro, Truro, Wellfleet, and the world beyond, but he wouldn't know it. For a moment, though, he distinctly heard that genial, toneless drone, humming, humming, humming, coming, passing, fading, dying back into luxurious drowse.

Now a deeply tanned, ragged drunk took lurching possession of the scrub pine behind him, in clumsy haste dropped his pants, squatted, fought to counteract his tilt, caught sight of Kozma, and spewed unintelligible gibberish—menace, or venom, or both.

Kozma would favor him with a bath if he sought to fraternize—likely get drowned himself, wash up on the breakwater for Vara to dispose of. O, fiascos now, thy names would all be shame.

The man lost his bout with gravity, toppled as a crepitating gush fouled Kozma's ears, angst of stink pursed his nostrils. Howls of rage, exasperation, revulsion, dismay, then loud and louder, more mettlesome, gleeful hilarity came rollicking at Kozma—the demand of woe to be heard, felt, honored. Kozma lifted a hand in salute to life's everlasting outrages.

The man answered with a grandiose groan, fished a little nip from his pants pocket, raised it briefly, sucked it down, lay back flat, and sighed off to sleep.

A couple went by laughing, his hand down the back of her pants, her head on his shoulder—they took no note of Kozma.

What was it all but illusion? Nothing would remain of him but Vara's memory.

Bravado, all bravado. Of course he was scared. He'd never died before. Nor ever would again. There was no encore, no getting rid of religion either, at least not in this millennium. Vara he suspected of becoming a secret Christian, her own kind, of course, a sect of one, neither righteous nor pleased with herself. He had mocked her mildly: "You should be a saint."

"I can't," she'd said—he thought a bit smugly—"I'm a Jew."

"Christ was a Jew," he'd said for the umpteenth time.

"The only real Christian, according to Nietzsche," she'd affirmed, as usual. "The best man who ever lived, the most humane—his father the worst god ever. After that what couldn't He ... what wouldn't He countenance? Holocaust and A-bombs. Entertainment for celestials. Nothing they couldn't stomach. The angels were right to rebel. They should have hauled them all off to hell."

"People are gullible," Kozma had said.

"The greatest man who ever lived," she'd insisted. "Kindness. Sweetness. Mercy."

"And the sword?" said he.

"Oh, the sword!" she'd said, long-suffering. "Did he really have a sword? Whom did he ever smite?"

"And the greatest woman?" Kozma had said.

"A million million mothers," she had said primly. "There's no pride of place for the likes of us."

He had smiled, conceding the point, touched as always by her love of Americanisms, himself having adopted an English accent.

Lately she had irritated him, trying to care for him. "Don't this, do that," too dear for his growing agitation and despair, his need for steel frightening her, as he became ever more irascible, cold and strange. Brokenhearted she seemed some days. Robbing her of his deathbed, or sparing her, how to tell? Both, of course. One can't control everything—one can control … nothing finally. Yet one must try. The mind has no freedom. Move my hand here, move it there—the bench is warm all over.

How could he? How can he? Because he knows she will forgive.

Lacking other modes he pled aloud, "Vara, don't forget me." For a moment whole horizons going to the gas obliterated time and place.

His caught breath let go again. His note to her was casual as a grocery list, as if she knew everything by heart and didn't need instructions, or miracles either.

Why couldn't he die in peace? He'd never been at peace. No peace in death either. Nothing's not peace. Nothing's nothing. Well, I don't want it.

Don't worry, you'll never know. Not yet. Not yet. Here you still sit, dripping sweat.

The ghost of Cervantes spoke: "With one foot in the stirrup, in the anguish of death, my Lord, I write to thee."

But Kozma was not in extremis—his anguish was mere initiation into weariness, pain, dismay, despair, fear of worse to come, which at least would set him free, though free he didn't want, only to live forever, childish he'd grown, senile. What worse disgrace?

Dismount. You're not dying, not even anguished, only despairing, and where was not despair? Don't desecrate the dauntless Spaniard dead the same day Shakespeare died—wait at least for that majestic date, April 23, so far, so far from here, while now he tolled the months in their glories on his fingers, seven of them, a reprieve, practically forever at his age, if he could make it half that far—his toll to be paid in full only then, whichever day whenever. He'd never get those damn sashes home, lifelong puzzle to their finder.

He would paint, yes, so he would, he would, he'd paint the sea. He needn't even glance at it, knew what it looked like, what it ought to look like—yellow-green streaks and streaks, all horizontals, an infinity of streaks, sun-gleams and white froth, nothing forgone, all said, his first and only abstract aberration, a parting wave to a path ignored, a broken oath self-pardoned. He'd painted the world (some of it); now he would honor the immaterial, befitting his immediacy.

Committing suicide began to seem more encumbered than he had expected. Just the preliminaries exhausted him. Valedictories occurred not, could not be summoned. Every milestone both triumph and defeat. Hope of escape sprang. He seized it by the throat, wrung it like a sour dishcloth, dropped it down time's cloaca—whither did it go? Nowhere. But it had existed, still existed, though fading in his brain, never to return, at least not often, or for long. All beyond grasp. Wondrous, wretched, outrageous, senseless, incomprehensible, not even tragic, even if the human race were blameless, inexplicable gift withdrawn.

Now, if ever, he must strive for some encompassment. Ignominious not at least to try. He wanted to stop and survey everybody that ever was, the Etruscans, the Lombards, the Merovingians, the tree-to-cave peoples, billions and billions—could it be billions? What futility, gone, unknown, forgotten? We too some day. Soon perhaps, should heedless human folly persist.

As when did it not? But now the human capacity to end life on earth was grown beyond conception or denial, unparalleled achievement. Banalities. Could he do no better than this? Was there really nothing left to say or seek? No new glimmer of anything? How could anyone die content without forsaking past and future both?

Twilight, and the last, the fast ferry, had already loaded at wharf's end—it must be what o'clock already? Already, that saddest of words or thoughts. He stood, abandoned his weights—who did he think would steal them? He might as well go see what he could see, so seldom a tourist, and never yet at his own demise. Why should he tamely sit for it?

A long, long hobble it was to the shining white ferry, immense, towering it loomed, hurting his neck to look up as he came near. He'd stiffened, yes, a perfect stiff he soon would be—well, a bit soggy, devoured by crabs, fish, squid, all the invisible mites of the sea, anonymous bones.

He'd worn himself out just getting here from home. He felt he'd aged ten thousand years on that anxious bus, but he felt again once and for all finally confirmed beyond any doubt in his determination to die today. He truly was a wreck, a derelict—high time to set sail, not a day, not a minute too soon.

Still, he'd loved it out here, when he first came to town, loved it with a landlubber's fascination. He couldn't remember the last time he'd scanned this ever-changing tableau vivant, the center of town import, constant cars stopping or not stopping to gaze, creeping in, creeping away, coming back again, unwearied, drivers exchanging commonplaces at the wheel, at a snail's pace moving on, making way for others, to repeat the ritual circuit not long hence—the Portagee Trail, he'd once heard it called—the harbor the be-all, the end-all of all things.

Who ever went to town and never had a look? Only washashores.

He'd spent his last ten years in his studio, lest he leave works unfinished.

Life was work—paint, better said. Always firm and correct he'd tried to be, as the I Ching decreed.

Strangely the gangway remained in place, not a soul in sight, no passengers, none waiting to wave, even at the huge, unglassed windows, all snacking inside, boozing no doubt, why not? On such a night, the stars coming into view, into vogue almost—it was eerie, though, like a ghost ship—only a very, very fat man, in simple fact a gargantuan man, and a very young woman, no, a pretty girl she was, in a pinkish dress no less, the very color of the emerging stars, suddenly conversed at leisure there on the float, all by themselves.

Where had they come from? Who were they? Ever less could he trust his senses. He often drowsed unknowing—wake, sleep, dream on his feet—how to tell? No longer so alarmed suddenly to find himself where? Why? Doing what? At home, at least, it mattered not, judging by Vara's forbearance, eyes never once askance.

Slovenly, too, Gargantua was, in voluminous black pants and a wrinkled, not lately laundered, half-buttoned white shirt, his black slab of hair toupee-like, not well stuck on—in one hand a large pastry he was leisurely biting, blowing away the errant flakes. No mark of identity or function—the girl's father? But where had she gone?

The black pants were ballooning as he toiled up the gangway, fastidiously wiping his fingers on a vast handkerchief, like a child's parachute strung with four stones it would have been and almost seemed as he started up some stairs within, disappeared, ten, twenty seconds later reappeared, right elbow leaning in a window on the bridge, left arm casually within, hardly attentive, effortlessly twirling the helm, doubtless with two fingers.

A half toot of farewell—perhaps to his daughter?—and then a swirling puff of black smoke like a big ball of barbed wire rose and dispersed in sparkles so brief he might have dreamt them, a mocking Christmas ornament. The ferry backed into the harbor, turned, and slowly, sedately glided away in rippleless silence, stood port off the deep-water buoy. A ribbon of white wake sprang into view, then seethed and burgeoned as it picked up speed, still perfectly silent in the last glow of fading light.

As Kozma stood alone at wharf's end, the only one to see the ferry lights vanish around Long Point, the melancholy of departures overwhelmed him, darkly chill in their desolation. He wanted to go, he wanted to stay. Only he remained, only he understood, blasé all others, while he longed with unbearable poignancy to be aboard, even with no ticket, not a nickel on him, no shred of identity. He wouldn't jump off, he'd engorge the whole voyage, jubilate the whole night through on a vagrant bench on Boston Harbor. Immortal reveries would exalt him.

Instead he felt lost and empty, deep in mourning for all things past or passing. Hopeless sterile night stopped his mouth.

Starting back to his bench and weights, he remembered where his precious pills were. Of course, of course, where else? Well, he wouldn't forget them again, now that they were out of reach, vain and useless. He should have known he'd remember soon or late.

But no, no, no, not out of reach. Elation—home again, home again! The dry exit he'd devised, so hard worked toward, was coming back to life. So he needn't drink his death, after all, not drown. That unwarranted dread was gone, forever gone. Cold vodka and sleep, sweet, well-earned sleep. She'd wake to find him gone beside her, as planned.

No, no, no, asleep, asleep, dead in his chair, note in his hand— where the hell had he left it, what said? No, no, yes, the second letter. What had he said in that one?

Dear God, which letter? Was there a third? What had he written? Inadequate, shameful, selfish. Well, back on the infernal bus he must go, or had the last bus gone? A taxi. More humiliation. He'd walk if it took all night. But what time had she told him she'd be back? Noon? Plenty of time. For what? Was there money in the house? There must be. In his wallet, which was where? What did he need money for?

Now, God help him, he remembered, too ... the pills, the pills, the pills, no longer lost, all the same were stowed in an awkward recess with ingeniously interlocking chairs he could hardly lift or reach at the time, more barricaded than hidden, now perhaps, no, now most likely, almost certainly irretrievable by himself alone. He'd forgotten he'd need to dismantle his impenetrable bulwark. He'd need Vara to help him, stronger than he was now, poor little thing. How he'd love to have her again, as in their green years, to know and feel all of her in full all over all in all, one last long embrace. Sex be damned, just to hold her in his arms—so hold her, what's to stop you?

Anyway, anyway, there should be an innocuous, unobtrusive splint for such doleful, inevitable occasions. Another chance missed, oh, a millionaire inventor he might have been, friend to all who lived too long. Or a firm, clasping, supremely thin condom, inflexible once one's member had been safely dropped in.

Everlasting fame and gratitude, towering monuments worldwide, his paintings doubtless forgotten, painted over, gone to the dump.

Oh, the real, the real, only the real is real, though what, pray tell, is that?

Suicide was more fraught, more arduous than he had imagined or braced for, all in all not so wrenching as he had feared, an adventure, almost. And him with time yet to kill. A suicide attempt a day would keep despondence at bay, so long as one kept failing. He seemed to have that knack at least. Despondence! Contemptible term! Comical almost, were it not spoken in earnest. So much the worse.

Some kids were diving and swimming, all chattering at once, challenging each other, dark-skinned kids, townies obviously. They looked to be ten or twelve, diving from the wharf itself, ten, twenty feet above the water, perfectly unselfconscious, indifferent, even somehow unaware of him, as if he had no existence but in his own mind—it occurred to him that he was dead, already dead.

Legs aching, short of breath, he stood to watch. What better had he? What better was there, in any case? The kids were calling on each other to dive, but one girl in particular was the object of their common voice—a poignant plea it sounded. She in acquiescence finally climbed from the water up to the wharf in the least suggestion of a bathing suit—two strings, three little triangles sun-faded and colorless.

Without hesitance she climbed a clutch of three pilings bound together with cable, without visible effort shinnied up the tallest, which rose another five feet, and then, by some trick of agility too quick or deft for the eye to catch or recall, she stood upon its flat top, a ten-inch diameter thirty feet up, the others suddenly silent.

She loitered about—to the terror of Kozma, too paralyzed to shout, to beg her down—turning both ways like a figurehead of the whole compass, looking off everywhere, hand on one cocked hip, a queen surveying her kingdom, and then without warning flew straight down, hardly a foot from the piling, like a cormorant, gone in the least little sprite of white froth.

Her companions seemed to think little of it, merely confirmed in her supremacy and their pride, but Kozma, watching her wring her hair, caught a glimpse of who they were and where he'd been for thirty years. Turning away he blessed them with his atheist cross, convinced they'd saved him—from what he knew not, nor cared.

His time was not yet ripe, not quite. People still passed—ten, was it? Eleven? It didn't matter. Time meant nothing now. The tide still had a way to rise. Midnight would come. The lights of the immense parking lot were on, and everything glared like noon.

At first he had feared to sit down on the edge of the walkway—which was what he'd wanted to do all along, sit and dangle his feet like a boy, but had fought off the urge, lest someone guess his intent. Now he was pantomiming to fish with no line, seeking to catch an audience, fooling no one, not even himself. He wanted to address the world. What would he say, what could he? The sash weights waited for him behind his bench. The drunk had apparently moved on, or crawled deeper into the bushes, or taken a hint from him and gone to the bottom.

Awaiting impulse and a clear coast, he felt himself drifting, as if unmoored. Funny if he fell asleep, fell in and drowned, save him the trouble of winding himself round and round with window weights. He was a boy in a summer field of tall grass and wildflowers. Unseen insects sang. The hill sloped as he followed it down into shadow, hoping to find his way. Darkness grew; the sun drew back behind him. He thought, I'll lie down here and join them, so long despaired of, so long, so faithfully kept from mind. And yet, here they were, where it was always summer among the leaves of childhood. Cool, kind shadows spread, dimming the light. He looked about for Vara. Sleep, he thought, she'll be my sleep among dreams of my family, I can feel her hunting for my hand.

Some thought like a wing brushed by. He knew he mustn't let it slip away, and turned to see.

A girl had come to sit with him, a girl with a hectic, scarred face—recent razor slashes they looked to be, hardly healed—in a short skirt, purple flip-flops, and an old sweatshirt with a logo too faded to read.

"Good morning," she said in a shocking voice—old and young both, kindly and wise.

"You must be an angel," he said. "How did you get...?" He gestured between them. "We're like two Frankenstein monsters."

"Oh, you're not," she said. She kept smoothing down her skirt, as if obsessed. "I lost my panties," she said to his wondering eyes.

"How...?" he said.

"Oh, I always do. I think I must like crazies."

"You must be more careful," he said.

"Oh, I know," she said. "Would you like to fuck me?"

"Oh, my dear," he said, more shocked yet, yet somehow not distressed.

"You don't have to," she said. "I'll suck you for a place to sleep. Or ten dollars, whatever you care to...."

"Oh, my dear," he said. "My dear girl. I haven't a cent. I'd gladly give you...."

"Oh, you're broke, too," she said.

How stupid to come off with no money, the only thing anyone ever really needed. "Oh, my dear child," he said, helplessly, hopelessly, "I wish...."

"You're not going to jump?" she said gravely. "You've been sitting here forever."

"No. No. No. No. I won't," he lied. "I promise."

"Lots of people off themselves these days," she said sotto voce.

"My dear child...." he said.

"Please don't mind," she said. "If I can get some money I'll come back," and she was gone behind him like a dream.

He got himself up to his feet, twisted to look for her, cork-screwed and groaning, but she was nowhere. He went and leaned on the back of the bench, looking everywhere. He knew he needed a cane, had resisted Vara's insistence, too proud even to try the highly polished, gnarled black one she had brought home, when? Months ago.

The parking lot seemed all people and cars, remote in motion, coming, going, traipsing through, voices calling back and forth, sounds of revelry, distant music, a can rolling.

Three huge, opulent motorcycles revved together, a sudden thunderous wall. One, two, three, and they blasted off as one, deafening, eclipsing all, vaunting, even at half-voice, vaunting, vaunting all.

How appalling that he had to die. He'd never really objected to death before. He felt furious now. If he were still a Russian he'd *be* furious. What Russian girl could possibly act like this, and still be chaste? But she was, she was.

He hobbled among the rows of cars, angling toward the shuttle, stopping every few yards to look around, breathing from the mouth, phlegm thick in his throat. He hawked, dropped a clot on his toe, swallowed, kept clearing his throat, trying to cough his voice free.

Desperate, he tried to hurry, wanting to shout, Stop. Where are you? Has anyone seen her?

Who among the blasé pleasure-seekers would hear, who would answer? How to describe a hectic girl with a scarred face, in a short skirt, purple flip-flops, and no panties?

Only in mad America, he thought. He would, he realized, give anything, anything, anything to find her, find her and give her a shower, a meal, a bed, and wait for Vara to come home. She'd know what to do. He could die another day.

The Bed

◇◇◇◇◇◇◇

I was scheduled to sit with some guy—door number three in a sprawling, labyrinthine house overgrown with Virginia creeper, inside like an abandoned campsite, sink piled with dishes, wrinkled jackets hanging askew in a closet with no door, clothes heaped in one corner—not unlike my own sordid abode—plus the musty smell of spillage and stale air, the scatter of pill bottles and an elegant, long-stemmed brass pot pipe I might well have snitched had I not quit all vain props and resorts.

Mr. Cold Turkey was I, lest I forever sink from depth to depth, the light gone to dusk, gone to dark, gone beyond me to pen my own name, much less an apt epitaph.

The guy at the door seemed frantic to be off. All I knew was I had a three-hour shift to kill, till the next volunteer freed me to resume my restless peregrinations, which would end only with me back at my own window nook, drowsing till the dawn gulls yelped me back to abject consciousness.

"He won't need anything," the guy said. "He's done with meds. Give him a glass of water if he asks, get him the piss bottle if he needs. Mostly he just sleeps. Trouble, call this number."

He thrust a scrawl of paper at me and fled to his due perdition, I hoped, for not leaving me the guy's name, though what after all could it matter?

Respite from my endless docket of chagrins was not so much won or found as forced on me by the outlandishness, the sheer defiance, the mad chutzpah of this household nonpareil. What remained of its living space—beyond the meager kitchen and dining area—was filled almost entirely by a gargantuan bed that bespoke a mode of life I had never met with, a communal dream, I suppose, it must have seemed, to some. It was—if I may surmise—a sort of designer playground, a vast mattress, maybe eight feet by eight, set in a mahogany frame some five feet high with no headboard or sides, just a vacant expanse of a single, soiled sheet upon which a skeletal wraith in an equally un-fresh johnnie lay curled up, seared by lesions, reddish, purplish, a hideous mauve.

I approached with circumspection to gauge how far this wretch had gone on his road to ashes or worms. Wispy-bearded, fleshless nose bone, cheeks caved in—he looked dry and hot as hell itself.

Dispassion, not pity, is my native pith; still, it gave me a twinge of remorse to have no thimble of dew for his tongue, whatever his deserts. Twilight had dimmed the low-ceilinged room. The windows were curtained with what looked like black velvet, the atmosphere so dense, so humid and stifling, it should have been wrung out and hung in the sun.

Edging closer, I heard a groan.

Startled, I said, "Yes?"

"Piss," came a whisper. I glanced about for said bottle, steeled to perform my pittance of use, however perilous or repellent.

He groaned with a note of strain, then again, sounding resigned.

"What?" said I. "What?"

"Too late," he breathed.

"Never fear," said I. "We'll get you cleaned up."

"Can't move," he whispered.

"Never say die," said I, inveterate my penchant for inapposite wit.

From his superior vantage he seemed to smile.

"*Permisso*," I bowed, but found no ladder, no steps—perhaps to keep him quarantined? An outcast? A one-man plague? That could hardly be.

And yet, what did I know?

Finally I climbed up on a rickety chair and then with perhaps reckless stress upon my general debility managed to swing a leg up and over, hauled the rest of me after, crawled to his side, and with no little distaste divested his person of its not very fresh . . . nightie, I'll call it.

Bare-naked as on his first birthday—there was no top sheet, not that it wasn't oppressively warm—he had not a ring, not a bruise, not a tattoo, nothing to rest the eye on, no cosmetic for his ghastly sarcomas, his emaciated buttocks worthy of Auschwitz, his shrunken dick, which had gotten him confined here, now meek as a mole.

Dear God, what a morass! Good works for whose benefit? Mine? To make me think on the plight of others? What preposterous presumption to send me here! What did I know of AIDS anyway, except that half the men in this mad town had it, while the other half were trying to get it in solidarity with those who'd got it already. Oh, the guilt of good luck! Better anything than loneliness!

I've learned to look elsewhere, never intrude in private misfortune. Everyone has enough of their own. And here was I, my abysmal self no less, absurdly out of place, my personal reformation barely begun. It occurred to me suddenly that I was in a very cauldron of due disaster. How many men had been infected here? How many had died, or were dying still? I realized that this was almost certainly his house, his bed, his social parlor, himself unregenerate to the last, his caregivers staunchly indulgent.

Or maybe they were all doomed, or already dead, him abandoned and bereaved, this the scene of his final, fleeting farewell to himself and his besotted pastimes.

Oh, bourbon, bourbon, bourbon should balm with kind solace this garish day's end. Ah, yes, jettisoned, too, my lovingly stocked, faithfully maintained pharmacological larder, gone to the dump with all ease of heart and rest of mind, gone all hope of mitigations, gone, forever gone . . . unless . . . unless . . . perhaps . . . maybe . . . I might just . . . just . . . just one soupcon. . . .

Shut *UP*! Shut *up*! Yes. Gone. Gone forever. And ever. Amen. Braced, however briefly, by this latest conquest of my ever-resurgent urge to revert, I let myself belly-slide down off the bed without breaking my neck, untucked the sheet all around, and grasped it in fistfuls.

Jaunty in my new role of Samaritan, I said, "We'll get you cleaned up in a jif," and pulled, but instead of the sheet slipping out from under him, or him rolling off the other way, he came along with it, sighing feeble apology. He was pure cumbersome deadweight, only his eyes alive with will to assist, or encourage, or at least not impede, or so it haply seemed to me. Useless, of course, utterly useless—all the same, a token of moral support, a sign he wasn't about to take death lying down.

I went round and pulled from the next side, and then the next *and* the next, but each just settled him back where he'd been, in a veritable vale of urine. And the sheet, the vast, odoriferous sheet, too, was saturated. He must have languished there some while. Nor was I, by then, what one would call dry.

This grotesque ghetto, in truth, revolted me, and how not? Doctrinal zeal, foment of risk, defiance of fate, perverse bravado, romance of doom, and I weary—weary and wary. Why must I attend here today, hardly fit to care for myself, much less anyone else, less yet for adepts of prearranged orgies. I should crawl into a hole and hibernate till things got back to normal.

Ah, normal, and what, pray tell, was that, and when, and where should one seek? No first kiss, I suppose, will ever after thrill the same.

Suddenly—I know not why—I remembered a foggy November midafternoon two or three years ago, when I first came to town. I was haunting the maw of the A-House alley, wanting some steps to sit down on or an overhang to hunch under, but everywhere was drip-dripping, and I was too wasted to bumble about glass cases in some die-hard emporium of tasteless trinkets or snatch a catnap in Marine Specialties among crowded racks of army-navy surplus duds aspiring to chic. Bars were verboten; I'd worn out my every welcome—not, I must admit, from obstreperous merriment, but merely for comatose states requiring conveyance elsewhere, anywhere but there, wherever I happened to be at that sodden moment.

A flow of well-dressed people was hastening by and swept me along. A man took my arm and steadied me through a chain-link fence and down a narrow cement walk across a vivid, emerald lawn, then up some wooden steps beneath a tall steeple, a neck-cracker when I bent back to reckon its height—the Unitarian Church it was, new to me then, the one with the Pilgrim murals and the baptismal font full of condoms.

I poured myself into a pew, fell asleep, and awoke amid a huge funeral, mourners crowded around the edges or sitting in the aisles, leaning over the balcony. The deceased proved to be a prestigious, popular charismatic, and many and many, mostly young men, were queued up to speak a few words—less, it turned out, in salute to his tireless work for gay rights, than in lengthy, ever more hilarious depictions of his martinet nature in bed, his tyrannical rule over precisely how and in what order all things should proceed—most particular he was, not easy to please.

One blushing young fellow followed another. In his dotage—if dotage it was (he had suffered no virile decline, au contraire)—in recent years this dignitary had enjoyed among this small populace as many suckers as had tumbled to Gaëtan Dugas in his transatlantic ... shuttlecockings, shall I call them?

Eulogies begun in hesitance soon convulsed to giddy heights of glee vying for vaudevillian supremacy. All constraints succumbed to hilarity at his amorous punctilios. I confess I found them eye-opening, having never shared a man's bed, and truth to tell, darn few women's since losing my family, alcohol being anti-aphrodisia to me.

I digress? Not at all. Memory simply broke into my cave of stupor. For who do you think was the amiable man who steered me to that exorbitant rite, and then drove me home, both of us the whole way howling with mirth? Never thought of since—there in the drenched bed reposed his specter, gone from vigorous manhood to wisp of viral ravages, while I drank the oblivious years away.

And did he recognize me? I at least was unchanged. Well. A bit gaunt, perhaps. No doubt. Yes, a trifle gaunt.

Crass familiarity, I suppose, to say, "Oh, by the way, you once took me off the street when I could hardly stand, and gave me a much-needed nap and an unforgettable glimpse of a world I would never have dreamt of." Well, they all looked most companionable, though in the dark how could I tell one from another, or, in the light, who was with whom?

And where was he now, behind those closed eyelids?—perhaps entranced in some happy dream hug with the very guy to whom he owed his destruction, the two about to become one in simultaneous quiescence.

Ah, romance, cheap romance, will one never tire, never be quit of it? And one, pray tell, who was he? Ah, yes—me, myself, and I. Author manqué. Mr. Logorrhea, who wrote and wrote, and never finished a thing. Why? Because he knew damn well the damn stuff was no damn good, mortal as he was, nor could he bear for shame to let his wife or anyone else see a single line of it. He got so jealous he couldn't stand to read living authors, so debased he'd take a bottle to some movie he'd never heard of, totter out as the credits rolled, confirmed at least in the superiority of his work to film.

In fantasy he could transfix a grandstand of sages, astound all with his quicksilver gift. But in truth he kept far from the real world of letters, especially the Fine Arts Work Center's preoccupied Fellows. Even with a second or third drink in hand, he could never approach to a word with any of them. He kept on the fringes, as if idly half-glancing in.

How at this distance can he know who or what he was—every page eventually reviled, torn to shreds, burnt, buried, shredded, or flushed to shameful oblivion, the hours of his head held in his hands?

He shirks the mirror, who once saw—or thought he saw—someone else, someone with a future. He knows too well now who's there to see, and looks no more.

He lost his wife and child, a boy now grown. He doesn't know where they are, Pittsburgh perhaps, where she came from, where he'll never set foot again. He couldn't face her family. (What *can* he face?) A better man surely stands by them now. He strives to hope so, while blinking away visions of a happy household. He knows "World's End"—what he calls this hellhole—will never sully their shining faces again. For that, at least, he's grateful.

While his poor, nameless ward here is steeped in his piss, too weak to move a muscle but his eyes, done with choice, alone with his terminus, that always- and ever-approaching mythical state he may personally never have meant to meditate, much less attend.

Suddenly amid my mullings I was relieved to realize that this unfathomable bed had a rubber undersheet—of course, of course. Blind until I see—a trampoline for pathogens.

I must find some surgical gloves. If I could get him down. If I could strip the bed. And the rubber sheet? Sponge? Mop? Towel?

It was no picnic but finally I got him unbundled, gazed upon a slimy, gleaming expanse of taut gray rubber, industrial tautness, with not a wrinkle, not a flaw but that single dimple in the middle, a patio of sorts, alas, with no table, no waiter, no drinks on the way, only my piteous acquaintance—I can't say adrift, but . . . far . . . far from dry land, call it haven, call it home.

But where had my efforts gotten him? Or me either? Or, for that matter, every last moment of my own wasted life? Near dead as he was though, and futile as I felt, I was damned if I'd leave him to languish up there in his puddle, irrespective of his deserts.

I tried to catch him by the wrist, then by an arm, but light as he was, and bare-naked, he was as slippery as a liquescent bar of soap, quick to squirt from grasp and slide away, like to sail off into thin air.

Once in motion, he wasn't easy to stop, or steer either. Impossible to get a grip on him, short of a full embrace, to which I was loath to commit. He kept slipping, sliding away, me circling the bed, gasping for breath, heart in my mouth as he spun like a runaway merry-go-round, always subsiding out in the middle, back in his pissy dimple, out of reach.

Panting, I paused to take stock—odd, but this felt like the hardest, the least likely, the most momentous test I'd ever faced. In those days my arm got tired just brushing my teeth. When my shrink advised exercise, I demurred that I could still hoist a glass—stein maybe not, but I don't suffer beer, never did, never will, and nothing now, come to think, nothing, nothing at all.

In the lull I strove for the jocular: "At least no feces."

"Not yet," he breathed, then quick to my leery eye, "A jest! I jest." Humor in extremis gave hope, at least of undefeat—which he seemed to affirm with grave and ready eye. But hope for what in cold reason? Not to be unmanned, I suppose. One couldn't just bawl, after all.

But even when I could reach him I couldn't get a grip, or even minimal purchase on the rubber sheet itself. I kept chasing, he kept sliding sideways, always like to fly off out of reach, glissading diagonals, my pursuit balked by bed corners and the constant need to reposition my wobbly chair. I could just see my neck getting broke while I was trying to do what, for whom?

Past humiliation, misgivings, and sense, I cast off caution—dignity I had long dispensed with as a bad joke—climbed onto my chair, heaved a leg up and over, and found myself once more on my belly like a seal, flippers flailing the slimy sheet (which would, in God's truth, have rebuffed ice ax or crampon).

Back upon that vast bed, once again eye-level with him, I had to face how frail he was, how intermittent his awareness, how feeble his efforts to help, how near gone he was, mouth slack, eyelids adroop, his emaciated length like a piece of slimy, dropped rope. I'd never been so close to the presence of death.

A kind of awe enveloped me—this man's end had come—then pity, then a terrible, intolerable fear, irrational, meaningless, immaterial, that all might go for naught, that he might die before I could get him down from that infernal bed, all my well-meaning goodwill, and his, too, snatched from us, all gone to loss.

Couldn't we just as well wait where we were, hoarding our strength, till reinforcements came? Anyhow, what was all this fuss about? Wasn't dead simply dead, nothing more, nothing else? Well, no, it didn't seem so, just then—more as if death were a greedy glutton I wanted to starve, for the nonce anyhow. I didn't want any help, either, I wanted to do it myself, with élan, no less, and no broken bones. And quick, before my relief came.

I flippered over to him, saw his eyes light, and got us gaily underway—you'll pardon. But of course, of course, haste is waste, or worse. Sudden speed, like a spring freshet, ice breaking up, surge of gravity—treacherous, the edges came flying. At every moment I feared he would sluice off aloft, and me with him, break his neck, break mine, mercy for him perhaps, perhaps for us both.

Glommed together, we spun and slid, dizzy whirligigs of disaster averted, more instantly looming, no way to slow down, much less stop, me shouting for maneuvers who could perform?

We were like to go sailing off onto tables cluttered with medical paraphernalia, whole pharmacies-in-waiting, this bed perhaps a communal hospice, and I, apparently, sole in command.

Where was everybody but just this one hapless soul I could neither get free of nor hold on to, much less steer—steer where, by what compass? Port Nowhere, away, away from edges, all edges, at any speed at all, but slowly, calmly, to slacken at last and drift, my toes adroitly ruddering us, scarcely breathing, till all inertia would one day expire, a chance come for us both to slip away to the floor, in tandem, with perfect ease and aplomb, venerable maestros at my special request gravely fiddling by ear Brahms' Quartet in A minor.

Well, no, no, just when it seemed we'd escaped our dread fate, we meanly careened, via centrifugal acceleration, our irresistible momentum gathering again, sparking alarms, prayers, paralyzed suspense; then there were sudden, secluded inlets, bays, a lazy leaf slowly, idly spinning while all seemed child's play, momentum sweetly waning to the languor of a pond in calm season, sails safely furled—but then by some unwitting budging of balance, no more than a cough, off we went again like a raft in smooth flood toward a high dam, all roadsteads astern, steep finales of falls speeding our way, rock-tortured white water, shark fins ahead, I hoarse from shouting, him sound asleep, or safely dead, who could tell? Well, how it was—he'd simply left everything to me. I'll never forget that, his complete confidence that I'd see to everything; I heard myself telling his family that he died at peace, with no regrets, thinking only of them. For a minute there I almost dissolved in gratified tears, when suddenly a noiseless door with no visible knob opened and a skeletal young man in a white johnnie shuffled in, taking no note of me, rustled around in a jumble of open boxes, found a handful of surgical gloves, and then painstakingly, with tiny steps, got turned round.

As the door closed behind him I saw a long, bare room with cots and young men like white phantoms lying or sitting or staring or edging about like sleepwalkers, without expression or sound.

I was appalled as never before; tears came down till I thought I'd drown.

Waking dream or hallucination, I've never told anyone, I wouldn't know how.

With new resolve I pursued him with my teetering chair, gasping for breath, till finally, like a fireman half-bellied in a window ledge, I caught a frail wrist, hauled him into my arms, toppled us sideways into space—one blank blink at world's end—crashed down to splintered chair and sprawl, him fortunately on top, both of us collecting an astounding coat of fur from the unswept floor, and I a fantastic goose egg on the back of my head.

He weighed no more than my shadow. Once I'd got him ensconced like a king on a throne of piled bedding, little puffs of breath parted his lips and pleated his belly—what little flesh remained.

Making naught of my piss-bedizened carcass, I could only shake my head and nod, till I too got to laughing with relief at having gotten him down, for what it was worth. He looked extremely pleased at his new elevation. All along he had seemed more concerned for me than for himself, all encouragement and approving eye. Next door to dead as he was, still he didn't want to see me confounded, didn't want me to be party to that fiasco. No, indeed! Nor would I in his place.

A granite block of a woman with a face like a pug appeared, glowered at me as an intruder in this select cadre of finalities. "How you doin' tonight, darlin'?" she said, and started putting things to right. Growling, she unzipped and dragged the cumbersome sheet to the shower, ignored the rest. Him in his utter nakedness she began to sponge with excruciating delicacy.

I gathered myself to depart, neither of them taking note. "Goodbye," I trilled with abasement, let my fingertips down to his chill cheek. He was weary, weary, but I thought I glimpsed esteem in his eye, and from her a circumspect glance.

Wonderment itself, I limped with slow tread home to my scattered room with its hot plate and minuscule cold chest, my shelf of imperishable foods, with nothing ahead but my empty cabinet where once no end of choice flagons of succor had faithfully waited to welcome me home from every last, latest despond.

Strange thing though—once I got showered and sat down again in my window nook with half a bottle of flat seltzer and a sense of exhilaration like I've never felt before or since, for a moment it felt almost remiss not to have croaked of my one and only date with the plague.

One fine, gallant fellow—I felt honored to have twice made his acquaintance, though little was the good I could do him on his verge of release. I was the doleful one, really, bereft of the chance to sit at leisure with him and gossip as if we were old cronies of infinite experience, parse past disasters, compare surprises, hopes, near misses, marvels, and triumphs, if any, of our blind sojourn here. We should have become fast friends of unfettered laughter; nothing could ever have fazed us again.

Ah, yes, and leaving that house I spied a mini-ladder under the bed. I never learned any more about him than I already knew—though

I think the world of him now, feel as if I've known him all my life long. A prince he is in my mind's eye, who helped me to help him die. That week I deferred all obituaries, loath to hold any one loss above so many.

Words, words, words are not truth. But what is?

Afterward, when things for me spiraled hopelessly down, I would think of us aswirl on that slimy bed, and laugh aloud not to cry.

I do these days seem to do nothing but cry. For myself, I guess. What a laugh!

Nor did I ever go back to that house that seems now no more than a dream, yet is all I care to recall of my last ten years. Still, thanks to my saving confrère of that epochal bed, I feel tolerably well armored for whatever's ahead.

But now, now what's to do? That wretched old question recurs, recurs. Surely it can't be enough just to steep life away in mere abstinence? Once I thought only the colossal could win fame and justify my wayward life, the unheard-of, the startling, the strange—no wonder they stymied me, those plots of interplanetary hoodlums with death rays, who would shrug if all earthly life expired of their depredations, cruel slavers from beyond the stars, galactic struggles for control of the universe, concoctions I couldn't have stood to page through myself, had I ever managed to finish one.

Since lack of drink has shrunk my tolerance for human proximity, and yet it seems I must live amid crowding retrospects, I see no choice but to embrace the solitary rigors of desk and blank paper, steel myself to start anew, this time with no booze, but only blood for ink.

Now I dream, when all my follies are plumbed, that I'll even know how and where to begin—of course, of course, in medias res:

"I went one day to sit with the dying. . . ."

for Helen & Napi Van Dereck

The World to Come

◇◇◇◇◇◇◇◇◇◇◇◇◇◇◇◇◇

Manuel Carlos was born in 1905 on the island of Flores in the Azores. Small, sturdy—hardly taller than a boy by our standards—dark-skinned, with a big nose, big shoulders, big hands, a deliberate manner, and a deeply furrowed brow and deep voice, he was more apt to shake his head than smile, though he was not averse to an occasional half pint of whiskey on a Saturday night.

He had come to Provincetown with his uncle in 1917, and had gone trap fishing with him until the uncle died in a gale in 1923, his chest crushed between his wildly pitching boat and one of the many wharves no longer in existence.

That same year he fell in love with a Cape Verdean girl he met at a dance. They were married almost at once so they could sleep in the same bed. A son with a full head of black hair—promise of good fortune, according to a widow versed in such things—was born the next year, the joy of their lives, who grew ever more handsome, grave beyond his age, an exemplary communicant of the church, who shed blessings and honor upon them, until his swamped dory washed up in a frigid December dawn just before Christmas, 1942, one week before his draft notice came.

After the first year, the expectation of another child assuaged their bereavement, but as the barren years went by and hope died, an aura of absence came to isolate all things. They passed their days quietly together, with mutual deference, shying from the garrulous intimacies and grudges of the West End, solaced by the changes of season, by observances of their faith, by tending their roses and vegetable garden.

For many years Mrs. Carlos waitressed at the Bonnie Doone. Otherwise she kept to her stove or clothesline, or stood at her fence or watched from her kitchen window for the infrequent passersby on their narrow lane at the end of Tremont Street.

At the demise of trap fishing, Mr. Carlos hired on with a dragger captain known for his even temper and prudence. The Carloses were frugal, and with the exception of a single visit to the great city of Lisbon, where neither had ever been, they seldom traveled or even crossed the bridge to the mainland. They looked forward to—then passed with muted satisfaction—the milestones of an end of house and car payments, but without any definite future in view. Life held no further anticipations, desires, surprises, or dread. The good Lord would see to them in time.

Mr. Carlos kept up with current events, saddened by local tragedies, awed and gratified by the progress of science. He got his news from radio, then television, when that came in, dismayed by the increase of public brutishness and the disrespect for patriotism that grew as the Vietnam War stumbled to its ignominious end. It hurt his heart to hear of people who, if they could, would not have chosen to be Americans. He avoided the teeming summer crowds in town, which grew larger and ruder every year, came earlier in the spring, stayed later in the fall, and behaved in ways Mr. Carlos felt sure—or at least hoped—they would not have done at home.

In due course he confessed he had fished enough, hired on as a part-time parking lot attendant, and bought a sweet little catboat from a young man in haste to leave town. On summer Sundays after Mass, Mr. and Mrs. Carlos would go for a sail with a picnic lunch, sometimes taking one of the neighborhood boys with them to Long Point. Proud of his English, Mr. Carlos would gently correct the boys' grammar and urge them to finish their schooling (and, if at all possible, go on to college); but, because he had done neither himself, his advice meant little to young men eager to get a place on a boat or join the navy or Marines, as their fathers and uncles had done.

Mrs. Carlos developed a weak heart and had to stop working. In nice weather they might be seen sitting on their porch—*deck*, it would come to be called, in the new lingo of tourism and grand, expanded mansions on the water—two little people, their heads just showing above the railing.

One day, as she was sitting there beside him, her heart gave a flutter, and she was gone.

Time stopped once she was buried. "Nooo, no," he'd say, "I'm all right, I don't mind being alone," and after a while the neighbors left him to himself. Every day he walked to Cabral's Market and got something for dinner or carefully drove his old car to the A&P for staples.

"Hey, Pard, how you doin'?" someone would say. "Doin' fine, thanks be," he would answer, and then they would talk weather. Occasionally he would park in the midtown lot and play cribbage or dominoes with the fishermen at the K of C or walk down to Flyer's Boatyard and listen to his contemporaries reminisce. He seldom spoke except to nod and affirm, "That's right, that's right."

In his youth, various nicknames had been tried on him, but none had stuck, and for the last fifty years no one had called him anything but Manny, a singular fact unremarked by his fellow townsmen, but one he took casual pride in, mixed with rue that he could think of no personal quirk or quality that he could rightly own and be known by, except *Sonless*, of which he didn't need to be reminded.

In 1987 he retired full-time; Social Security and his savings sufficed to keep him. He had neither needs nor wants. Every Memorial Day, after he had tidied the graves of his uncle and wife, and laid a rose on his son's barren plot, he would walk the great beach at high tide, as he had done twice a day for a whole week, by moonlight or howling gale, that December his boy was lost, never to be cast up by the sea.

Mr. Carlos was too humble, too proud, too incredulous to seek personal miracles, but he could never resist the impulse to stop and envisage his son rising out of the distance, rowing across the bay from Plymouth, where, somehow, he had been brought to dry land, there lost in amnesia till this very day, always a year deeper in the past.

Shouting his joy, Mr. Carlos would wade out to his chest in the swell. His son would ship oars to let the dory slow, then turn and stand with widespread arms to meet him—a boy, a young man of twenty, stranded in time.

Naturally Mr. Carlos had an eye for weather, knew well the deceptive atmospherics of the low hook of sand when scanned from bow or stern, at speed or slow, whatever the season, day or night. He felt strong in his common sense; thus was amazed to read in the *Advocate* that Jonas White and Beeza Blaisedell, coming back from a two-day fishing trip, rounding Wood End past midnight, had seen a spaceship near Wood End Light, so near in fact that it had blocked the lighthouse from view, at first causing them to think the red light was out. Two others had been aboard, hired from the Old Colony Tap for lack of help. Neither had ever been aboard a scalloper—or any fishing boat—till then. Mr. Carlos shook his head at that.

On Sunday—he had dismissed it all as foolishness—he began to see leaflets about a public meeting of something called Sky Watch, to be held Wednesday at the Community Center at seven p.m. He guessed he should go and see for himself what the furor was, but he felt reluctant, oddly lethargic, and couldn't seem to haul himself away from his TV and window chair—he seldom left the house after dark anymore—till finally with a grunt of resignation he rose, washed and shaved, put on a clean white shirt, folded the cuffs of his sleeves up just above his wrists, and left the house ten minutes late, walking very slowly, bent worse than usual, foreseeing the need of a cane but hoping to postpone that concession for a good while yet. He found the place cram-packed with natives and washashores alike, standing two and three deep around the walls, craning on tiptoe behind the crowded rows of chairs or sitting cross-legged on the floor up in front, where Beeza and Jonas, dressed as if for church or court, were sweating under the lights at a table on a makeshift stage, recounting their experience of last Tuesday, May 15.

"I never used to believe in UFOs," Beeza was saying, "but not anymore. It took maybe twenty minutes for us to get from the Race to Wood End, and I was seeing these bright flashing white lights all the way. When we got about a hundred yards off I saw a strange mass like I've never seen before. It wasn't a helicopter, it didn't have any wings. It was completely round, about thirty feet high by thirty feet wide, with a lot of windows around the top half. It was silver-colored or gray. I don't know if there were any people in it, or if they got out or what.

"When we got close I heard four booms and saw four more objects taking off from Long Point straight into the air. All I could see was a yellowish tinge of light as they shot up at about a thousand miles an hour, fastest thing I've ever seen. You wouldn't believe."

Someone must have said something Mr. Carlos didn't catch, because Beeza said, "We wasn't drinking or taking drugs, I swear."

Some people guffawed, then others joined in, whether they knew Beeza or not.

"I'll tell you on a stack of Bibles," he said. "All of a sudden they stopped in the air and flashed these bright, bright white lights. I saw three or four more of them buzzing around between Long Point and Corn Hill in Truro. They kept stopping dead still in the air and flashing those lights.

"It was scary. I wondered what the hell was going on. I don't believe in those things. Thirty years I been at sea."

"Twenty-five for me," Jonas said. "I've never been a UFO person either, but nothing I'm aware of can move like that. I been around that point a million times, but what I saw was what I saw, and it was big. It was definitely a craft between us and Wood End Light. It had more or less oval windows with light coming out, like a vehicle with its interior light on. We were both in the pilothouse, we had our faces glued to the windows. When we went by it didn't take off, but there were two or three other objects flying around over the water. The radar didn't pick them up, they were too fast for the radar, but they were there, I saw them. I was too freaked even to call the Coast Guard. We were some glad to get out of there."

Answering questions from the audience, they said the same but slightly different things in almost the same words, though they disagreed somewhat—Beeza counted as many as ten UFOs in all, while Jonas thought maybe only five or six. It was hard to keep track: they changed positions so fast, you couldn't tell one from another.

Then the north district ranger stood up and said the National Seashore's position on the sightings was an open mind, but it certainly would investigate any reports of suspicious activity. Flying aircraft would not be a permitted use. UFOs would be classified as aircraft and thus prohibited from flying any closer than 1,000 feet from Seashore property. Hovering too would be prohibited.

Someone called out, "Maybe you should post the area, like for piping plovers."

The ranger said, "I wouldn't know what language to use."

Another voice suggested a saucer with a red slash through it, and people laughed and cracked more jokes.

Mr. Carlos couldn't see much from his place in the rear of the hall—now he really could have used a cane to lean on—but he heard enough to get the gist.

A Wellfleet man said that back in 1975 he'd seen what he guessed was an experimental aircraft. "It was just one big bright light, yellow-white like a spotlight. It flew erratically as if it were in turbulence, then it flew in a straight line for a while, then it went into a tight zigzag pattern, and then it disappeared with a sound like a big jet."

A washashore woman said, "One night at Herring Cove last November my friend and I suddenly noticed a big star, except that it was getting brighter or falling out of the sky. It came lower and lower in a straight line, right at us. As it got close, we just stood there watching it. Even with a high wind and loud surf we could hear the sounds of a huge engine. It looked like an electric razor with the three shaving heads inside a larger circle. Then it came down to about a couple hundred feet and disappeared behind a dune. Then it came back with three smaller UFOs and another big one, and the five of them flew in a pattern with the little ones in the middle."

"Family night," a man said.

"We watched for about two hours," the woman went on. "They didn't move like airplanes. They went back and forth and up and down. Or they stopped and stood completely still, then off they'd go again."

"Struttin' their stuff," said a dark-skinned man.

"We weren't frightened," the woman said. "We thought it was great."

Mae Bush yelled, "I'm hoping one of them will show up tonight. If they ever come down around me I'll jump on and say, 'Take me, baby.'"

"You would," a man shouted. "But they wouldn't."

Amid more laughter another woman called out, "Spotting some intelligent extraterrestrial life might make the summers seem more sane."

An impatient, reproving man's voice said, "Obviously these craft are from a much more advanced civilization. They're just looking after us, they're our keepers. We're their larvae."

"They're not doing much of a job," a stranger grumbled to Manny. "Larvae! We're not insects."

"No, we're not," Mr. Carlos said.

"Might as well be to them," another man said.

The ranger got down off the stage with Beeza and Jonas, and the President of Sky Watch stepped up and said, "From the response we've gotten, we know people have seen these things for years but have felt unable to talk about it. People have been ridiculed and told they don't even exist. It's time to respect the people who've seen them and give them our support."

A Wellfleet man interjected that for ten years he'd lived on a high hill overlooking the water, but just this winter he had started seeing lights doing strange antics. He had stopped counting at a hundred sightings, and this summer he planned to conduct boat tours of the areas where he'd seen the lights.

"You'd think they'd need a traffic cop up there," a man said.

The Sky Watch woman said, "Evidently other-world visitors have become fond of the Outer Cape. Interest has been so high I can't keep up with the phone calls. For those who don't believe, I have just one piece of advice—anyone can see them. Just go out there at night and look.

"And now," she said, "we're fortunate to have with us perhaps the most prominent UFO investigator in the world—artist, author, and Wellfleet summer resident Budd Hopkins."

There was scattered clapping; her head disappeared from view and was replaced by one with bushy eyebrows and big glasses. "My own experience with UFOs began in 1964 in broad daylight," Hopkins said. "I was driving on Route 6 and spotted a small, circular, metallic craft. I followed it for two or three minutes, driving very slowly, and then it zoomed out of sight. That event changed my life.

"For the past twenty-six years I've been documenting the stories of people who say they've been abducted by aliens and have undergone physical examinations and medical operations, which appear to be genetic experiments on the human reproductive system, and may indicate that the aliens are attempting to crossbreed with humans.

"I know—to the uninitiated, this must sound shocking, but...." He paused. "It *is* shocking. Of course. Can we have a show of hands of those here who have had UFO sightings or have experienced abductions?"

To Mr. Carlos's astonishment, about a fifth of the audience raised their hands. He wished someone would ask how many had actually been abducted, never mind the sightings. He was even more amazed when Hopkins called to the stage a Truro woman, whose family Mr. Carlos knew, who told of her ongoing abduction experiences, recovered with the help of hypnosis. She remembered as a child being in a spacecraft with "moon men," as she had thought of them. They had her convinced they were her friends. She said she had marks on her body similar to those reported by others who had been abducted.

"I'm scared of the night sky now. It's beyond human logic. People here know me. They know I'm not a nutcase."

Hopkins said, "I've been in touch with between 400 and 500 cases of people with recurrent experiences of missing time and psychological trauma—something disturbing about their past they can't explain. They have low self-esteem and trouble trusting themselves or their relationships. Self-doubt and suicide are common. The daily dose of pain I get isn't pleasant. It's very difficult for these people to come forward and recall their experiences. I salute their heroism, strength, and resilience.

"This is a worldwide phenomenon. Abductees' drawings of aliens are extraordinarily alike—little stick limbs with hands and fingers, huge black eyes in a huge head on a very thin neck."

"Snap it right off," a man muttered.

"They seem to communicate by telepathy and may even be able to read human minds. That may be the most frightening thing of all—that and the increasing incidence of UFOs all over the world."

Identifying himself as director for the Mutual UFO Network, a man said, "You talk with enough people and you can get into a situation where you don't sleep nights. Those who are less comfortable with the idea of alien encounters may feel reassured to learn that those who have had encounters had them first in childhood. Those who have not had encounters before adolescence won't be the subjects of inquisitive aliens. I don't know whether that will make you feel better or worse."

Hopkins ended by saying that from time immemorial human beings have stared into the sky and wondered what's out there. "The old answer was the gods, but now we're beginning to have some new answers. People with higher levels of education are more likely to accept the possibility of other life elsewhere.

"In any case, if experiments on humans are taking place—and I have every reason to believe they are—the world as we know it will be forever altered. A sea change will occur. The stakes are high."

A free-for-all of commentary ensued. A man said, "They're just getting us used to them, they don't want to panic the whole planet." A woman said, "UFOs tend to concentrate near whales, the oldest mammals on earth, because their development allows them to study and communicate with the cetacean population, which may be the wisest on earth, and fast diminishing besides."

A man challenged this last, and a woman shouted that whales would remain an endangered species for as long as the human race infested the planet. Another voice said with acid scorn, "Obviously the human race is a self-endangered species."

A familiar WOMR voice said, "In assessing the credibility of what you've heard tonight, your feelings will tell you more than your brain can."

Mr. Carlos felt bludgeoned by talk, cramped from standing in one place, craning his neck to catch a glimpse of the speakers. With a sense of complete bafflement, he made his way out the door, almost hesitating at a Sky Watch table where people could sign up. He had never signed up for anything in his life, and it didn't make much sense to start now. Fresh air was what he craved. His back ached, and once outside he half-sat against the low retaining wall to rest and regain his mental bearings.

Shortly everyone thronged out, all talking at once, laughing, calling to each other as they went their ways, sounding jubilant to Mr. Carlos, like a football crowd leaving a game won by the home team against an old rival.

Matt Silva, Eddie Gaspe, and Tony Coelho spied him by the wall, looking a bit weary and corkscrewed.

"What d'you say, Manny?" Eddie said. "Seen any lights lately?"

"No," Mr. Carlos said, rather gruff.

Matt said, "We're going to the Old Colony, have a couple of beers. Want to come? I'm buying."

"That's very kind of you," Mr. Carlos said. "But it's getting to be my bedtime."

"All you do is stay home, Manny," Matt said. "We never see you from one year to the next."

"Stay home all the time," Tony said, "you get old."

"I'm eighty-five," Mr. Carlos said, "if that's old."

"Jesus," Matt said. "I didn't know that. I've got to buy you a whiskey. You sit right there, I'll get my car."

"Now you're talking!" Tony cried.

Mr. Carlos was pleased to be included, eager to hear their views of the meeting, abashed but glad to be helped into the front seat of the car, then to get a pull out of it, right at the door of the OC, never having been helped anywhere before, his back tonight the worst he could remember.

They got settled in the east window, where the benches didn't tilt so much. Matt went to the bar. Eddie followed and got the four bottles of Budweiser, and Matt, walking gingerly, brought four brimming little glasses of whiskey.

"Canadian," he said, setting them down. "Good for what ails you."

"If you came out more often, Manny," Tony said, "we'd drink a damn sight better."

"May you live to a hundred and ten in good health," Matt said, lifting his glass, and the three younger men toasted Mr. Carlos.

Natives all, all had been on the water once. Now Eddie Gaspe drove trucks for Ducky Noons; Tony Coelho worked for the cemetery department; Matt Silva was a mailman.

"Thank you, thank you," Mr. Carlos said, adding gravely, "No one knows the hour, God keep us."

"Amen," Matt said. He was a natty dresser with a meticulously trimmed black beard, turning silver. He had never gone beyond high school but early on had taken a shine to history. "It's just a hobby," he would say, but if you had a question about the past he couldn't answer on the spot, he'd have more on the subject than you might want to hear next time you ran into him.

"So, Manny, what d'you think of that Beeza and Jonas?" said Tony. Hoarse from smoking, tremendously lanky, in youth he'd damn near broke his damn fool neck trying to kick the ceiling in the Fo'c'sle. The abiding mischief and heedless energies of those hard-drinking days had maddened three wives and countless girlfriends. He was a boarder now in his unmarried sister's house.

"Sounds like something's going on out there, wouldn't you say, Manny?" said Eddie.

Bantering and bluff, he looked about as wide as he was short, for four years the first-string high school fullback, whose wife had disappeared years and years ago, leaving him with two boys to raise.

"Hard to believe," Matt said, "harder not to—after tonight. They can't all be liars or kooks. No one could make up things like that."

Tony said, "Nothing new about lights at least, we've all seen plenty of them out there, probably lights out there when the Indians were here, didn't make no never-mind to them."

Matt said, "I doubt they ever saw any flying saucers, though. I wonder what they'd've thought."

"Shot 'em full of arrows, if they had any sense," Eddie said, "eh, Manny?"

"Probably giv'em food and water, like they did us," Tony said.

"Hospitality!" Matt said. "We better hope it's not payback time."

Eddie said, "We wasn't there."

"Sins of the fathers," Tony said.

"I don't think so," Matt said. "They don't seem hostile. Just curious."

"Christ Almighty," Eddie said in an odd voice.

"A mouse ran up my nightie," Tony sang in falsetto. "Bit my tit, made me shit. . . ."

"No, no," Eddie said. "I just remembered something I musta heard a million times. In the family. My grandfather—listen to this, Manny—he and his dory-mate got lost from their trawler in a dense fog. Anchored all day out there, they couldn't see two feet, no voice left from shouting.

"They gave up and sat to wait it out, till a strong current set in, nasty cross sea cobbled in amidships, so they had to bail. It got so bad they finally had to up anchor, let go God knows where. All of a sudden they heard a big steamer coming right at them. They hoisted mast and sail and hailed Mary as loud as they could, which was nothing but two whispers. It loomed out of the fog right at them, but slow, engines down to nothing. Next thing they knew they were up on deck, dory and all.

"Captain says, 'Good thing you showed that light.'

"Granddad says, 'What light? We din't have no light.'

"Captain says, 'We saw a light on you just in time, otherwise you'd be splinters in Davy Jones's coffin.'

"So, what they figured was, it was a phosphorescent gleam of the sea that broke against the dory's side. Out there in the middle of the fog. Nobody really believed it at the time, but that was all they could think of. Now I got to wonder. What that light was."

"We used to call that Providence," Matt said.

"God's wand," Tony said. "You think He's keeping watch on us? Out on the bank? In a fog?"

Eddie said gruffly, "That's what they teach anyway. I quit worrying about that a long time ago."

"What d'you think, Manny, God keeping an eye on them aliens?" Tony said.

Manny nodded slightly, slowly, more in acknowledgment of the question than in agreement, while his mind veered between phosphorescence and UFOs.

Matt said, "I suppose they could be the new gods, like the Greek gods that lived on Mount Olympus, and came down to meddle in human affairs."

"Looks like they can do anything they want," Tony said. "Come and go. Study us the way we do ants."

"But what they want, and why they're here," Matt said. "*That's* the question."

"You think they're here to help us?" Eddie said.

Matt said, "We could use a little saving. Right about now."

"I thought Jesus did that," Tony said.

"Needs doing again all right," Eddie said. "You think they're like a warning? Like a heads-up. Shape up or ship out."

"Doesn't seem like it," Matt said. "Maybe they *do* want to cross-breed with us."

Eddie said, "Why'd they want to do that?"

"You got no self-esteem," Tony said. "We're better-looking than they are—at least Manny is. You ever been abducted, Manny?"

"Not so's I noticed it," Manny said so seriously they all had to laugh.

"Some of these good-looking gals," Tony said. "Wouldn't you, if you were one of them extry-triestials?"

"Maybe we're not attractive to them," Matt said. "You'd think they'd take people back to where they came from, the way the English did the Indians. Like Squanto."

"Where's where they come from?" Eddie said.

"Hey, Pard, right next door in some other dimension," Tony said. "Maybe they're going to take us over to their side, show us a good time. Never send us back."

"Never say never," Eddie said. "I want to be buried and et by worms the way nature intended."

Matt said, "I doubt these . . . celestials . . . pay much heed to nature. As we know it. They've probably got a nature of their own, bigger than ours. What do they want that we've got and they don't?"

"Like I said," Tony said. "Women."

"Maybe they're not men," Matt said.

"So what are they?" Eddie said. "You think they're women? Hermaphrodites?"

"Something else," Matt said. "They don't mate or anything like that. They're past evolution, if they ever had any. They create and maintain themselves out of materials that don't exist on earth. They have no feelings, no pain, they're all brain, no emotion. They're pure calculation of how best to perpetuate their existence, and do whatever it is they decide to do. They have sciences we can't even imagine. At least that's what I get when I try to scope them out. Maybe they just explore."

"What worries me," Eddie said, "is do they have a conscience? I mean like ours?"

"I don't know," Matt said. "For them breeding with us might be like Adam and Eve tasting the apple. Maybe they just want to be happy."

"Like us?" Tony jeered.

Eddie said, "I'm not sure I like this kind of talk."

"Too spooky for you?" Tony said. "What d'you think, Manny?"

They waited for once, each curious. Years ago he had heard something that helped him envision God's majesty—that there were more stars in the sky than grains of sand on earth—and once, right after his wife died, he had dreamed of himself as a boy and the girl he had just married holding hands under a dome of diamonds, but suddenly, familiar things seemed a teeming blur, like a TV gone haywire. Finally he admitted, "I don't know."

"Neither do we," Matt said. "We're just talking."

"Sometimes you got too much imagination, Matt," Eddie said. "I almost wish I hadn't come out tonight."

"Almost don't count," Tony said, "so we forgive you."

"Think a minute, Eddie," Matt said, "think how much we'll know in a thousand years, compared to now."

"Don't make me laugh," Tony said. "How many years you giving us? Fifty? A hundred? We're too stupid and greedy. We'll be back to eating each other."

"Are these ... things ... under God?" Eddie asked.

"Omnipotent, omniscient, omnipresent, and perfect," Matt said. "Creator and ruler of the universe. Maybe these beings come from another universe and have a different God, maybe one that'll banish ours, the way ours did that pagan pack."

"It's the same God everywhere," Eddie said.

"Yeah," Tony said. "Everywhere around here. What d'you say, Manny?"

Manny shook his head gravely.

"You think they're going to take over?" Eddie said.

"Who knows?" Matt said. "Not tomorrow anyway."

"Makes me mad," Eddie said.

"What've you got to be mad about?" Tony said. "They haven't done anything to you."

"I don't know," Eddie said. "Freezing my ass off in Korea. Wipes everything out, sort of. The government should do something."

"The government," Tony scoffed, "is worse than them UFOs. You wait, they'll be taking our fishing rights away one of these days, just like the National Seashore took the dunes and back shore—I used to drive my buggy all over out there, the wives and I. Best times of my life."

"So," Matt said, "what are they?"

"Some kind of mental epidemic," Tony said. "Ball lightning, will-o'-the-wisps. How should I know? I don't believe any of it."

"Yeah. Hey," Eddie said. "Let's talk about something real for a change."

"This is real," Matt said. "We were there."

"Yeah, but we weren't *there*," Tony said.

" I do know *one* thing," Eddie said, rolling his shoulders and cracking his neck.

"Yup," Tony said. "I got two burials tomorrow."

Matt said, "Manny doesn't have anything to do tomorrow. He can figure it all out for us."

Eddie and Tony cleared the table. Manny hobbled to the car with Matt, was helped in, then out at his door, grateful for their solicitude, but he didn't at once climb the steps to his low porch. He waited till the car was gone, then made his slow way down to Sal's wharf and picked a path in the dark through the litter of sailing gear, oars, shingles, cinder blocks, oddments of whatnot in milk crates, till he reached the end, leaned upon the railing, and looked out at the bay.

It was a perfect night, cloudless, clear, sweetly cold, with a sky full of stars. His eyes at least were still good, for which he gave thanks, but there was nothing unusual to be seen, and he grew sleepy. He thought, Tomorrow, when I haven't drunk myself down, I'll drive out to New Beach and spend the night on watch.

This he did, nights on end, over the next few years, and saw many and many a light—the high jets heading for Europe; planes stacked up over Logan, or planes taking off; refractions of water and clouds; lights that appeared and moved slowly, steadily in a straight line out of sight; fishing boats coming home, or going out; the beacons of Plymouth twenty miles across the bay; but nothing like what was reported that night at the Community Center.

He scanned the newspapers faithfully, studied all he could find about the UFOs of Cape Cod, but it was only a dying echo. In time the hullabaloo slipped from mind. When he mentioned it at Joe's Barber Shop or Dyer's Hardware, people would squint to remember and then amiably bear with him for a minute or two, but for them it was one of the many mysteries of life that did not affect them personally. Others were simply hostile to the subject, or bored by it, or saw it all as optical illusion, natural phenomena, anything but beings from other galaxies. In recent years fewer and fewer people he knew seemed to remember anything about it at all.

Increasing solitude, so much brooding, weighed on Mr. Carlos. He thought, I must be getting old, but I don't feel old, just stiff in my joints and sore in the back. Never having known loneliness, or looked for anyone to ruminate with, he went on talking with his wife before sleep at night. Sometimes he heard her voice, but whatever he said, he always knew what she would answer.

One last time, standing alone and alert on the great beach from midnight till dawn, he strove to welcome explorers from other worlds, offering himself to the sky. He didn't know how or what to say or do, think, plead, or pray. He could only yearn with nearly uncontainable excitement for the vast mystery to be revealed, after which nothing on earth would ever be the same.

He felt selfish, seeking special privilege, but he so fervently desired to live to see the new world dawn that he felt it would be remiss beyond pardon not to strive with all his remaining strength to witness the greatest advent of all time—excepting the birth of Jesus Christ, he reminded himself.

By turns, therefore, as strength failed or revived, he resumed his vigils, arms spread wide, palms up like the poster of an Indian sachem in full headdress that had stirred his earliest awe and sense of rue, chagrined now not to know the man's name or tribe.

Mr. Carlos did not dwell on old words like *fortune* or *fate*. The sea encompassed all that. Eventually age forced him to sell his house and go into the Manor. He could not help being surprised at his physical decline, but his mind, thanks be, still felt strong. And once he had settled in, everything was done for him, and he had nothing to do between waking and sleep but think about the world to come, nor had he ever needed much rest.

His friends came to see him now and then and tried to interest him in anything but space and time travel—the town was changing; the fishery was ailing; ten-wheelers no longer rolled off MacMillan Pier for markets in Boston and New York; the gregarious Foc'sle bar had sunk to a plain eatery, no more an all-purpose social center, poets' corner, or office, working-class hangout, source of gossip, gripes, tall tales, job ops, irrepressible hilarity, legendary binges, all presided over by the near-unfailing indulgence of bartender-in-chief Mike Moon Henrique and his inviolable jukebox.

Summer houses once rented in the off-season were bought up and renovated; they stood empty in the moribund winters. Piggy's and the dance bars vanished, as did Cookie's Tap, the Portuguese redoubt in the West End. Daytrippers and weekend crowds dwindled after Labor Day, once the sweet, cheap season. Everything now was high-end tourism, skyrocketing rentals, the giddy glee of real estate bonanzas—Don't take down that For Sale sign, just jump the price 20 percent, 30 percent, 40 percent. Longtime year-rounders slipped away silent as the fish—nothing the same, someone said, but the tides and a native eye for weather.

Mr. Carlos couldn't grasp the fading aura of immemorial things, the rueful shrugs and head-shakings. With resignation, his friends would nod and repeat all the reasons for the shocking departures and dour postmortems.

Nor were there any more otherworldly visitations. Matt strove to reassure Mr. Carlos. "We know what we saw. We'll be seeing these darn things again someday, and for a long time to come. And a long time gone, too. It seems there are paintings of what look like flying saucers in the Renaissance, in prehistoric caves, in pre-Columbian cultures...."

"Hey, Pard, you sneaky ol' cuss, you been at the library again!" Tony crowed. "What else you dug up?"

"Lots of sightings. All over the world," Matt said. "Hundreds, maybe thousands. Other governments don't deny these things exist, just ours."

"They're not very friendly," Mr. Carlos said. He seldom spoke, except in answer to direct questions, and never in such a dire, aggrieved tone. His friends gaped at him.

"It does seem they don't show us much consideration," Matt agreed.

"Why should they?" Tony said. "We're puny compared to them."

"It's our planet," Eddie said.

Tony said, "When these buggers come they'll take us over with telepathy. They won't even have to lift a finger. We'll be like zombies."

"Cosmic karma," Matt said.

"Are we back to talking about this?" Eddie said.

"We're just kidding," Matt said.

"Trying to stay awake," Tony said.

"If they're supremely intelligent," Matt said, "I have to believe they're good, not evil."

"Why so?" Tony said. "Some of the worst people I know are smart as hell."

"Just my instinct," Matt said. "Otherwise nothing makes sense. Human sense, that is."

"Why should anything make any kind of sense?" Tony said.

"I leave that to God," Eddie said.

"He'll take it under advisement," Matt said, "I feel pretty sure."

That was Eddie and Tony's last visit. Matt still came every few months. Retired, wife dead, daughter married in Utah, son gone to wanderlust, he felt a bit as if he'd adopted Mr. Carlos, who had no one. He never chafed at their palaver, nor ever had a thought beyond those he'd already voiced.

After the first few minutes, everything summarized, nothing accepted as certain beyond what they had witnessed at the Community Center that night, they would sit in silence, musing at the hilly green cemetery of lichen-grayed gravestones tilting every which way, the newer, neater ones, like little replicas of modern blocks and buildings, complacent in the sun.

In total absorption and perfect accord, they dwelt upon the old days and ways, the gaudy dawns and fiery sunsets, the kind of darkness densely flecked with light, the gift of the stars, the ever-changing seasons, the faithful boats, the storms and miraculous survivals, the stunned losses and memorials, the end-all and be-all marvels of the sea itself, merciless in its infinite grandeur and beauty.

Always they parted with profound affection—and then no one came.

In profound seclusion, Mr. Carlos felt like an alien himself, possessed by an eerie sense of imminence. His fellow residents had no purpose, were not even waiting to die, but Mr. Carlos kept striving to live to meet the first space voyagers to find the planet earth.

Some nights, wearied in his vigil, he would steel himself with an Indian war cry come down from some lost swamp battle up Cape two hundred fifty years before: "Hold fast! Ootash! Ootash!"

It's only a matter of time, he exhorted himself—tomorrow, or the next day, or the next, if only I can keep myself alive. Breathe, breathe, keep breathing, and breathe—while on his watch, which slid up and down his age-spotted wrist, the second hand jolted from mark to mark, round and round the changeless chain of a day's twice twelve numbers, daunting to dwell on, impossible to forget or ignore.

Mr. Carlos's ardor never died. He thought only of beings from infinite distances with inconceivable existences and unknown motives, benign or brute or indifferent, perhaps merely curious, like himself, something like himself.

But not human. And how many kinds of beings inhabited the universe or possibly endless universes, beings perhaps not vitalized by life at all, but by unknown means, their vessels, in some other dimension, powered faster than the speed of light, beings perhaps immaterial, virtually immortal.

One of a tumbled stack of donated magazines told him that recent astronomers had designated 10,000 stars, some much larger than our sun, but knew not how many more might exist beyond human ken, perhaps an infinite number, or even an infinity of other universes, each with its own galaxies of infinity. And Mr. Carlos himself was what? A human being, he had to allow, both puny and titan-like. After all, the ants too were real, well ordered and magisterial in their colonies.

Mr. Carlos had long since ceased to pass more than commonplaces with the harried priest, who contained storms of terrifying struggles with his nemesis, gin, and was disinclined to intrude upon a soul of such monumental equilibrium that it seemed to verge on the uncanny.

One day in tongue-tied desperation he dropped his forehead to Manny's bony shoulder, aghast. He straightened up instantly, felt not shame but the psychic flow of strength and solace, recalled a late contemporary, who used to say, "You take the holy where you find it."

In departure he tried inconspicuously to go to one knee, lost his portly balance, nearly toppled, had to laugh. "Thank you, Manny," he said.

"Thank *you*, Father," came the predictable reply.

Mr. Carlos had never talked back to his uncle, had never failed in devotion to his wife and son, had lived, so far as he knew, a wholly moral life without effort or regret, with exceptions so few and minor that he could not recall them. Heaven and hell had come to seem minuscule corners of earthly fatality. Once he caught himself feeling sorry for God, and did not deem it sacrilege.

His life of bereavements melded into anguish that he had been born too soon, and must miss the apotheosis of human history, one that would make nil of all previous knowledge. And what would happen then?

Sometimes Mr Carlos despaired of reaching the future—one moment he felt strong, the next vacant and adrift. Throughout the ages, all had died in ignorance, even the seers and saints—but not, he now saw, in *this* ignorance, this *new* ignorance that knew itself to be the brink of revelation—and unless far travelers revealed themselves soon, so would he. And then . . . even that might be but a glimpse, with eons, perhaps infinite eons yet to traverse to behold the origin of all things, did such states as beginnings and ends even exist.

One day, waiting in the sun, scanning the *Advocate*'s meaningless news, he came upon the obituary of Matt Silva, dead at age sixty-eight—a fall from a ladder.

He sat unmoving for so long, and then was so unresponsive, that for a moment they thought he might have had a little stroke. One of the nurses noticed his finger pressed to the heading in his lap.

"Oh," she said, "I'm so sorry. That's your friend that used to come. I always thought he was your son."

Grief cast Mr. Carlos out of mind: he couldn't grasp why he felt so desolate and bowed down, till he remembered that the lights came no more. Whatever they were, they'd learned all there was to know about the planet earth, or they'd found the human race needless of further study, an odd thought that once had shamed him. But now, in all solemnity, he felt the same. What did human marvels amount to, more than mere survival of time?

In his distress, Jesus came to sit with him in commiseration. Mr. Carlos recognized him as his own son, never to be reborn, and did his best to comfort him. They nodded together, side by side, muffled and remote. The skies swarmed, but they couldn't lift their eyelids.

One year a nurse asked him if he'd ever been married, and he had to ponder.

"Course he was," cried a white-haired nurse, big as a barrel, glaring at the younger one. "She was a fine woman, too."

He knew there had been someone else, but the ache slipped away. Bent nearly double in his wheelchair, Mr. Carlos went on shrinking and darkening. A kid saw him parked by a window in a shaft of winter sun and with the poet's delight in semblances blurted, "He looks like a walnut."

"Scat!" a nurse snapped at him. "Go bother your uncle."

Afraid Mr. Carlos had heard, she asked if there was anything she could do for him. There was not. He thanked her earnestly, in his invariable way, now hardly a whisper. She bent and very gently reached with fingertips to touch the back of his vein-large hand.

All the other residents were called by their first names, but not Mr. Carlos, who was everyone's love for his native courtesy and indestructible dignity, so self-contained and always so grave.

He died in his sleep in the year 2003, age ninety-eight. It was a commonplace day at the Manor, withal a sad one. There was no one to notify. "Who was he?" a new nurse asked. Several were standing around condoling.

"He was an old-timer here," one said. "He worked in the parking lot."

"He was a fisherman," said the big white-haired nurse.

"Well," the other said, "I distinctly remember him in the booth downtown."

As one offended beyond all possible excuse or recompense, the old nurse cried out—fierce, exasperated, bellicose—"For Chrissakes! He was a fisherman!"